STAGES OF GRACE

CAREY HEYWOOD

Carey Heywood LLC

Stages of Grace
Copyright 2013 by Carey Heywood
Cover by QDesign
Edited by Yesenia Vargas

All rights reserved. Except as permitted under the U.S. Copyright Act of 1976, no part of this publication may be reproduced, distributed, or transmitted in any form or by any means, or stored in a database or retrieval system, without prior written permission of the author.

The scanning, uploading, and distribution of this book via the Internet or via other means without the permission of the publisher is illegal and the punishable by law. Please purchase only authorized electronic editions and do not participate in or encourage electronic piracy of copyrighted materials. Your support of the author's rights is appreciated.

Stages of Grace is a work of fiction. Names, characters, places, and incidents are either the product of the author's imagination or are used fictitiously. Any resemblance to actual persons, living or dead, events, or locales is entirely coincidental.

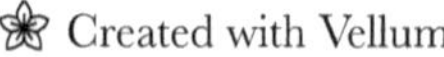

Stages of Grace

Denial, Anger, Bargaining, Depression, Acceptance...

When facing death, a mourning period is to be expected. But what if it's not a person but a relationship that dies? Grace and her boyfriend Jon have been together for three years. They live together and have shared many beautiful memories. Those memories are what keeps Grace from admitting Jon has changed and is no longer the man she fell in love with.

Afraid of being alone and holding on to something that no longer exists, Grace is a shadow of her former self. Her daily objective is to hide her pain from the world. Then, an unexpected letter sets off a whirlwind of potential life changes. In life, sometimes the hardest thing to do is let go.

For my Emma Grace, never settle.

Denial

a psychological defense mechanism in which confrontation with a personal problem or with reality is avoided by denying the existence of the problem or reality
-Merriam Webster

Sometimes I wonder if the past I'm trying to preserve was even real. That it actually happened and I haven't created this fantasy in my head of what we were. We were good. We were happy.

I believe it so fully I can almost taste it, like that one perfect bowl of ice cream topped with whipped cream and pears that I shared with my father at an out-of-place French-style bakery that closed its doors only months after opening. Jon and I were happy once, and the certainty of that fact, the memory of what we were, was the only thing keeping me from…From what? Leaving? I had nowhere to go.

It was a Thursday, the day the doctor's office I worked

in stayed open until seven. That with my forty-five minute commute gave me the hope that maybe, just maybe, Jon might be out when I got home.

Five minutes from home, I turn the radio off. I'm not sure when I started doing this, but the silence calms me, helps me prepare. After maneuvering into our assigned spot, I glance up at our second story apartment. My shoulders sag when I see the light on in the front room. He's home.

After killing the engine, I sit for a moment, listening to the random pop and hiss from the engine as it stills. Maybe tonight will be different, maybe he'll be back. It's cold out, and the inside of my car is already noticeably cooler. Collecting my things from the passenger seat, I hurry up the walkway to the stairs that lead to our second story apartment. I take the stairs slowly, looking out for any slick spots.

Before putting my key in the lock, I force a false smile, opening the door with a cheery, "Hello, honey."

"You're late," Jon is sitting with a book in the leather armchair by the sofa. The TV is on, but the volume is barely a hum.

My smile falters. "It's Thursday, Jon."

"I know what fucking day it is, Grace." Why does my name sound like a curse? Jon stands quickly, forgetting the book in his lap.

I watch it as it falls to the floor, his place lost. "I only meant—"

"Oh, I know what you meant. You think you're so much smarter than me." Jon reaches down to retrieve his book and storms back to our bedroom.

I stand there, the pounding of my heart a roar that slowly fades as my breathing stills. I hang my purse on a hook by the door before walking into the kitchen to rinse my Tupperware lunch container. I keep one eye on the bedroom door and the stream of water low as I do this in case Jon comes back out.

As I set it on the drying rack, I catch myself looking around the apartment, thinking back to a time when I was so happy here. Jon had been let go from his job the year before. Before that, I had been so certain we were happy. Now I wasn't sure if I knew Jon at all.

He was originally from New York, that's where his family still lived. After he lost his job I know he wanted to move back, but he stayed in Cleveland for me. We met at a bowling alley. I was on a disaster blind date and was trying to figure out a good excuse to end the date early. That's when I saw him.

I can still remember how handsome I thought he was from that first moment. He was tall, with wide shoulders and short dark brown hair. He had a strong jaw and the bluest eyes I had ever seen. He was captivating. He had been bowling with a group of friends a lane over from us. When my date got up to go to the bathroom he caught my eye and said hello to me.

The maroon and gold plastic chairs of his lane backed up to mine. He was sitting in the corner chair, the one that looked straight out at the pins. I was sitting facing the other chairs. His arm was slung over the chair behind mine. When he said hello I jumped, and his fingers touched my arm as he apologized for startling me.

The heat from his touch felt like a brand, like he had marked me. When he asked if my date was my boyfriend I groaned and rolled my eyes telling him it was a blind date. He leaned back in his chair, crossing his arms over his chest and said I was not the kind of girl who should be going on blind dates.

I had asked him what he meant by that, and he moved

over to the chair right behind me and told me blind dates were for girls who didn't get asked out face to face. Jon was charming and talked me into leaving my date that night for him.

When my date came back Jon told him that we were old friends from high school and asked if it would be okay if I hung out with him to catch up instead. My date seemed relieved, and when he left there was no talk of another date. Jon left his friends, and we sat at a small table by the bar. I could still picture us. My hair had been longer then.

I cut it not long ago, excited to try something different. He flipped. I had never seen anything like it. Full-blown anger, over hair. When I started crying, Jon apologized, pulling me into his arms. Moments before, I had felt so beautiful with my stylish new haircut just shy of shoulder-length, I had been so excited for Jon to see it. I was growing it back out now. It was taking a long time, but it was now past my shoulders.

My eyes flick back to the bedroom door, and I exhale when I see the light is turned off. He's gone to sleep. If I am lucky I can slip into bed without waking him and be gone to work before he woke the next morning.

Tomorrow is Friday. Most people who work during the week will be thrilled and greeting each other with "Happy Friday." It is my least favorite day at work because it means I will be home Saturday and Sunday.

I used to live for the weekends, for curling up with a good book or taking a day trip somewhere fun. Nowadays, weekends seem like staring contests until Jon finds some reason to scream at me. It doesn't even matter if I am playing his game or not.

It wasn't like this the first month Jon was out of work.

He had still been actively applying for jobs and doing extra chores around our apartment since he was home during the day. Jon would cook elaborate dinners and go buy flowers for me. He would meet me at the door with a kiss and ask me how my day had been.

Now, he had barely talked to me in months. After that first month, his severance package ran out. Still undeterred, he continued applying to places with the hope of some response. He managed to get called back three times that month for interviews. Each time, he heard nothing afterward.

With my job I was barely able to cover our apartment and my car payment. Jon filed for unemployment when it became clear that without it his car was going to be repossessed. He was on unemployment for six months until his claim ran out. Ever since then, Jon had become more hostile and withdrawn.

I learned the hard way that certain questions would set him off. Had he applied anywhere? Had he heard back from anyplace? How was his day? These were some examples of potential minefields. I slowly stopped initiating conversations to avoid setting him off.

It seemed as though even hello wasn't safe anymore. When his car was repossessed last month, it had been especially hard. Jon was so angry, and the only one he had around was me. Three months into his unemployment, he had stopped talking to any of his friends. I was the last thing he had any sort of control over.

I ate a sandwich and set my plate in the sink to wash the next morning before going into the bathroom to wash my face. There was less makeup to wash off these days. Jon had accused me of "painting my face to try and find a new man." Since then, I had just about stopped wearing any.

I was thankful I wore scrubs to work as Jon could not find any fault with those. Every day, scrubs, insulated Crocs, blonde hair up in a tight bun, and almost no makeup. One time, washing my hands in the bathroom at work, I had looked up myself. It seemed as though I had aged ten years overnight.

I grabbed the pajamas I kept in the bathroom and quietly changed in there before turning off the light and going to bed.

Jon was on his side of the bed, his back to me. I slowly eased into bed, careful not to disturb the sheets or comforter. I slept on one side, my back to his, holding the edge of the bed. It seemed almost impossible for there to be any more free space between us. It was hard not to think back to the days when our love was new and exciting.

From that first night at the bowling alley when Jon had come up with a plan to convince my date that we were old friends and that I was going to stay with him so we could catch up. I could not even remember the name of the guy I had been on a date with. I could only remember Jon.

Jon's plan had worked; my date had left, and Jon had ditched his friends to buy me a beer at the little food counter. I had no intention of letting him take me home, I was going to have a girlfriend swing by and pick me up. Jon was fine with that.

He just wanted my telephone number so he could call and take me out sometime. I can still remember how attracted I was to him, how my stomach flipped when he had asked me to stay with him. I still hoped we would return to those days.

The buzzing of the alarm on my phone wakes me the next morning. I hurry to turn it off before it wakes Jon. When he moves I freeze, holding my breath until I hear him rustle again, exhaling when it is clear he is still asleep. I rise slowly from our bed and tip toe to the bathroom. I take my shower, then get dressed.

After pulling my wet hair up into a tight bun, I brush my teeth and walk out to the kitchen. I pack my usual frozen lunch and a yogurt into my lunch bag and grab a granola bar to eat in the car for breakfast. After slipping on my Crocs and heavy winter coat, I take my purse and keys off of the hook by the door and quietly leave the apartment.

In the past I would race down the stairs to my car and start it before running back up the stairs and into the apartment to wait while it warmed up. Ohio winters sucked, and I dreamed of the day I could afford a remote starter. These days, I waited in my car while it warmed up because of the one morning coming back into the apartment I had woken Jon up.

I had been standing in the foyer giggling because I had just completed some Olympic-level maneuvers on our slippery stairs and had somehow managed to not fall on my ass. Jon came roaring out of our bedroom, screaming at me for waking him up with the door and then my giggling. I had stood there sobbing, trying to explain, trying to apologize. It didn't matter to Jon. From that day on, I waited in my car.

As the car warms up I wiggle my toes to keep them from feeling so stiff. I have the defroster on full blast, and once the windshield and back window are clear enough to see out of, I reverse out of my spot and drive to work. We live in the suburbs of Cleveland. My office is closer to downtown. My favorite part of the commute is crossing the Cuyahoga River. The river reminds me of my parents.

As I approach the river I make sure I'm in the slow

lane. Each morning, the river looks different. The trees lining the banks shed their last leaves weeks ago, the water reflecting the bare branches above. Some mornings, I can barely see the water as a swirling layer of mist obscures it. Something about the river centers me and has a calming effect. The fact that it is also the part of my commute where my toes seem to thaw out may also have something to do with it.

When I get to work I start my computer before grabbing my water bottle from my desk and taking it and my lunch bag to the break room. After putting my lunch bag in the refrigerator, I'm filling up my water bottle from the cooler when my co-worker Nikita comes in. Nikita is twenty-two and somewhat of a partier. With her come the obligatory big plans for the weekend question. I have no idea why she still even asks. Maybe it is out of politeness, but either way, my answer is always the same.

"Nothing, do you have any plans?"

"I was thinking about checking out this new wine bar. One of my girlfriends went there last week and said it was fun. Or there's that new movie coming out, you know the one with that funny girl who won the Oscar."

"That sounds nice." I add, and it did.

It's been so long since I've done anything fun like that. Single pretty girl that she is, Nikita always seems to be doing something interesting. I can't believe how much older I feel considering I'm only twenty-five, twenty-two seems like a lifetime ago. Nikita chats happily as she follows me back to our desks.

The office will be opening shortly and so will the phone line. Between the both of us we cover the patients getting checked in, making photocopies of insurance cards, updating addresses to manning the phones and setting new appointments. I'm thankful our office is busy. It keeps the time to chat down to a minimum, and I feel better when I'm doing something. The only downfall is it seems as though the days fly by, and I'm back in my car again, headed home.

Jon will definitely be up tonight when I get home. He will also be expecting dinner. The days of him cooking are long gone. I put my hand on my neck as I slowly roll my head from one shoulder to the other. I get my now empty lunch bag and purse from under my desk and walk out with Nikita. She is still happily chatting without a care in the world while I, on the other hand, move slower with each step, almost willing my car further away.

Resigned to the fact that I have to go home and that Jon will be there. I slow as I cross the Cuyahoga, wishing for the peace I feel when I look at it. That feeling of peace leaves me once I'm past the river, replaced with a dread that builds each mile closer to home I drive.

Parking the car, I look up at our apartment. It had once been a place of so much joy. When Jon brought the idea of officially moving in together I had been thrilled. We had been dating exclusively for almost a year since the night we met at the bowling alley. I had been thrilled.

We had basically been living in my cramped studio apartment for the last six months. It was decided, Jon would move out of the house he shared with his buddies, and we would find a place to rent together. The complex we settled on was halfway from both of our jobs. It meant a little bit longer of a commute for both of us but not by much.

Our apartment felt like a castle in comparison to the tight squeeze of my old place. We had so much fun decorating it and making it feel like home. I had felt bliss there at one time. Now all I feel is as though I am walking a tightrope suspended over a deep canyon with no hope of making it across.

No, I shake my head. We are fine. We are going to get through this. I love Jon, and he loves me. Everything will be okay. I unbuckle my belt and gather my things before carefully making my way up the walkway, then the stairs. False smile ready, my key is in the lock.

Looking up at me from the leather armchair, Jon smirks. My face already feels exhausted in maintaining my false grin, as though someone had said, "Say cheese!" before being ready to actually take the picture, and I am forced to stay there, just waiting for the shutter to click.

Jon's face shows no visible sign of being happy to see me. His eyes survey me, stopping when they meet my eyes and then drop back to his book. I hang my purse, keys and lunch bag on the hook by the door. The hook is one of three attached to a plaque that says Home Sweet Home. Shrugging off my coat, I hang it in the coat closet, then go to the kitchen to start dinner.

"No need to make anything for me," Jon says rising, his book now face down on the arm of his chair.

Now that he is standing I can see that he is neatly dressed, wearing slacks and a button-up dress shirt. I want to ask where he is going but know better and feel intense relief at the thought of him not being there. Nodding quickly, I look down. It is impossible to know what reaction I will ever get from him.

Currently, he seems indifferent. Jon must have been waiting for me to get home to leave. He puts on his coat and goes to leave. His fingers hesitate over his own keys for a moment before remembering he no longer has a car, and they move to take my keys instead. Part of me rebels within. Why should he get to take my car without asking?

Jon is out the door without saying goodbye or when he

will be back. It seems unfair that he expects me to account for my time when only going to and coming from work each day. He needs to blow off steam, my mind argues. Maybe when he comes back he will be in a better mood, I hope.

Still in the kitchen and now only responsible for feeding myself, I make a sandwich and sit down to watch TV. In an effort to save money since we are down to one income, I had purchased a digital converter box for my old TV since we could no longer afford cable. Sometimes I had to adjust the antenna, but it got all the basic local channels.

With my plate on my lap, I watch Jeopardy. When Jon and I first moved in together, we used to watch it every night while we flip flopped making dinner. We never kept score but would shout out answers, though never in the form of a question. We stopped watching months ago. I had answered a tricky question and looked at Jon with a big smile.

His response had been, "You think you're so fucking smart, don't you?" Taking in my wounded expression, Jon continued, "Great. Now you're going to fucking cry" before turning off the TV and storming to our bedroom, door slamming behind him.

We never watch Jeopardy together anymore.

Suddenly I feel paranoid for watching it at all, so I turn the TV off and go to clean my plate. Our apartment does not have a dishwasher. I can almost hear Jon's sing-songy voice as he would say, "you cook, I'll clean" when we talked about the lack of dishwasher.

These days, I do all the cleaning. There are a pile of dirty dishes in the sink that had not been there that morning. I cannot help but notice that there seem to be more plates than one person might use during the day. I wash them, placing them one, by one onto the plastic drying rack beside the sink.

I go to the bathroom to wash my face and brush my teeth before changing into pajamas and going to bed. It feels strange, having the bed to myself. I plop down into it without a care and take my time getting comfortable. Sometime in the night, I start when I hear the front door close.

I lie there, eyes shut, doing my best to appear asleep. Jon switches on the bedroom light when he walks in. Still, I pretend to sleep. I hear him walk over to my side of the bed and can sense him over me. He stands there for a few moments. I do not move an inch. With my entire being I wish him away. I almost open my eyes when I feel the feather light touch of his finger brushing a strand of hair behind my ear.

Was that affection? I am too startled to respond. As quickly as his fingertip brushes my cheek, it is gone. Jon turns off the light before undressing and climbing into bed. I lie there stunned, hopeful. Jon still cares. He has to. I drift back to sleep with a feeling I have not had in months: hope.

The next morning I wake early. I would have loved to sleep in, but I had gone to bed fairly early and have an internal alarm clock. Jon is still asleep so I ease out of bed to not disturb him. His touch the night before was still affecting me. I feel almost light and cheerful.

Wanting to surprise Jon, I quietly set to baking cinnamon rolls in the kitchen. It's my mother's recipe, and Jon loves them. I remembered my mother as I made them. My parents died in a car accident six months after Jon and I had moved in our apartment.

My grief had been so palpable at that time that Jon had been my one saving, well, grace. I was an only child and handling my parents' estate had been overwhelming. Jon had helped me sort everything out. My parents' house had been a nightmare to deal with.

There was still a mortgage on it, and due to the housing crisis in Cleveland, had been underwater in its value. I had a few nerve wracking moments with the bank holding the mortgage, but with Jon's help, was able to get everything squared away.

Cleaning out my parents' house had been especially hard. I saved photos and other memorable items. I felt such an overwhelming sadness that since I had no children or brothers and sisters or aunts and uncles that their memories were only known to me now, that their passing was only felt by me.

Once the estate was settled, I was able to pay for their cremations and the rest went to paying off my student loans and some credit card debt. Jon had been with me, holding my hand as I released my parent's ashes into the Cuyahoga. My parents had loved that river. Maybe that was why I did too.

I am just taking the rolls out of the oven when Jon comes out of the bedroom. Setting them on the stovetop to cool, I smile up at him. Jon moves past me to the fridge, ignoring the rolls, and gets a soda. I move my gaze to the rolls so Jon will not see my smile fade.

I make a plate for myself and take it to our small table to eat. Jon goes to sit in his armchair and turns on the TV. After eating, I wash my plate and go to take a shower. Jon walks in as I am about to step in the water, and I grab a towel to cover myself, startled.

"Don't worry Grace. You have nothing I want to see," Jon says, pulling a bottle of painkillers from the medicine cabinet before slamming the door closed behind him.

I stand there allowing his words to sink into my core. I

have nothing he wanted to see. What does that mean? How could I go so quickly from the most beautiful girl he had ever seen to this? As much as I want to turn the water off and curl up in a ball on the bathroom mat to cry, I don't.

I step into the stream of water. It is hotter than I expect, and I rush to turn the knob to add cool water. As I shampoo my hair and clean my body, I cry quietly, curious if the man I love will ever come back to me.

Those words become a chorus in my head: "nothing I want to see, nothing I want to see." I remembered the days when Jon could not keep his hands off of me. From our very first stolen date at the bowling alley. I had two beers with Jon. Afterward, as he waited with me in the parking lot for my friend to pick me up, he kissed me for the first time.

It was a September evening, and even though we were having a bit of an Indian summer, it had cooled off outside once the sun had set. We were sitting on the back of his car, looking up at the stars. Jon was making me laugh by making up names for constellations.

Jon pointed across me to a grouping of stars low on the horizon. When I looked back at him, smiling at his ridiculous name for them, I was not expecting his face to be right there. Locked in the gaze of the bluest eyes I had ever seen, Jon leaned in to kiss me. I had felt lit from within, as though every nerve ending on my body was emitting heat.

I was so surprised I had kept my eyes open the whole time. His lips were soft, and the kiss was sweet. After our kiss we looked at each other almost stunned. I wondered if he felt the same way I had. Our second kiss followed not long after. This one was less sweet and more of a promise of things to come.

I had been almost sad to see my friend pull up. Jon had

my number and promised he would call the next day. I traced my lips, feeling his phantom lips still on them. Claire, my friend and neighbor, teased me on the ride to our building. She had never seen me like this and was still stunned I had ditched my date for him. It had been completely out of character for me. Claire had seen Jon, so it was easy to see why I had been so taken. Claire was just hopeful he had some cute single friends for herself.

I dry off after my shower. Our bathroom does not have a fan for the steam, only a small window that I should have opened but didn't. The window is meant to vent the steam, but it is too cold outside this time of year. I use my hand to wipe condensation off the mirror and look at myself. Nothing to see now, and once I had been so desirable. We would get past this. I dress and brush my hair, leaving it down. Maybe Jon will be happy to see how long it is getting.

Jon is in his armchair when I come back into the front room. The roll I had eaten is the only one missing from the tray. He hadn't had one. Why not? I look at the tray and back to Jon. He's sitting with his head down, still reading. He had not even acknowledged I had come in to the room.

"I made rolls."

"Not hungry," he says. turning a page of his book.

"But I—"

Jon huffs and looks up at me. "Yes?"

"Nothing."

I hurry back to our bedroom and sit on our bed. Why am I so upset? My emotions are overwhelming me. I bring my hand up to cover my mouth as I quietly break down. I don't want Jon to hear me. I don't want Jon to see me like this right now. He must have heard me, though, because I look up, and he is standing in the doorway, coldly looking down at me.

"You're crying over some fucking rolls."

"I…I…I"

"You what?"

I just sit there shaking my head.

"Spit it out!"

Jon is yelling now and standing over me. I shrink further down, pulling my shoulders in, a sitting fetal position. He words a roar in my ears, I cannot understand him. Why am I getting yelled at for crying? It is surreal, almost as though I am watching from the other side of the room. His anger is now wholly directed at me. All I try to do is love him and support him. Why is he so angry at me?

Jon tries to lift my chin up, to make me look at him. I struggle to keep my face down, his fingernails biting into my skin, I want him to go away. I don't want him to see me like this. He throws his hands up in frustration and storms out, banging the door shut behind him.

From the bedroom I hear a crash in the kitchen and then the jingle of keys being taken off the hook by the door followed by the boom of the front door closing behind him. I want to go see what the noise in the kitchen had been but feel incapable of standing. Falling over onto my side, I pull my legs up into my arms and hug myself.

When I am all cried out, I go into the kitchen to see what Jon has done. The pan of rolls no longer sits on the stovetop. The pan is on the floor, and a sticky mess of rolls is everywhere. Instead of crying again, I start cleaning. I throw away all of the rolls, even the ones that had landed on the countertop and not the floor, telling myself I will never make rolls again.

Once the rolls are in the trash, I take a soapy sponge and begin cleaning the icing from the walls, countertops, cabinet doors, and floor. I notice right away he took my keys, meaning he probably took my car too. Where did he go? When would he be back?

Given the weather and being without my car, I feel trapped and stir crazy. I gather up our laundry and a roll of quarters, huffing it downstairs to the laundry room for our building. I lock the door behind me using Jon's keys. The machines are smaller than the machines at the Laundromat down the street and cost more, but I have little choice on foot.

Taking up four of the twelve available machines, I separate our clothes into two loads of colored and two loads of lights. I take out my book, Arrows of the Queen. I brought it down with me so I could sit on a stool in the corner of the room and read. It is a book I've read before but enjoy so much I reread when I have nothing else.

Thirty minutes and four dollars in quarters later, I move all of the laundry into dryers. I am lost in my book until I hear stomping and doors slamming upstairs. It's as the though the air is pulled from my body, a feeling of dread settles in its place.

Jon is home, and given all the door slamming, is angry that I am not there. I stand in the doorway, unsure of what to do. Leave the clothes and tell him where I am or stay with the clothes and let him stew? I hear the door slam again and heavy footsteps on the stairs. He is coming down.

I open the door and feel a blast of cold air. "Jon?"

He is halfway down the stairs when he hears me. Jon comes down the rest of the stairs and approaches me so quickly I automatically back up in the room until the wall is at my back.

"Don't you ever leave without writing a note again," he hisses in my face.

I look down and nod, wondering why he can leave

without telling me where he is going. The dryers' buzz indicate they are done. Instead of offering to help me carry the loads back upstairs, Jon turns and leaves. I slowly begin unloading the laundry into our baskets and then carefully carry them up the stairs to our apartment.

I am surprised to find the door locked and fumble to get Jon's keys out of my pocket. I unlock the door. Jon is sitting in the leather armchair. I almost ask him why he locked the door when he knew I was coming up with my hands full. I raise my eyes to his, and he lifts an eyebrow at me, almost willing me to ask that question.

I don't. Instead I look back down and pull the laundry behind me to our bedroom to fold and put away. It is barely mid-afternoon on Saturday. How am I going to get through another night and day of this? As I fold laundry, I think about the first time we did laundry together.

We were still living separately, and Jon had brought his laundry to my place for us to make a date of it. We went to a Laundromat near my old apartment. Jon kept me laughing by telling me jokes the whole time and stealing sweet kisses when no one else was looking. When our laundry was done we used the long tables there to fold our clothes.

I could still remember how embarrassed I was when Jon picked up a pair of my underwear with one hand and fanned himself with the other. It was still early on in our relationship, and we had not gone all the way yet. Jon wanted to. I did too, but I was nervous.

I snap back to reality, stiffening when I hear Jon clear his throat behind me. I am not sure what he wants and slowly turn to face him, eyes down.

"Grace, are you keeping something from me?" Jon slowly makes his way over to me.

"What? No," I say, confused.

"You haven't baked in ages and now you're doing laundry. I say someone has a guilty conscience."

"I just—"

"You just what?" he screams.

"Wa-wanted to make you happy."

"That's just it. You haven't thought about anything else but yourself and now suddenly you're thinking about me. You are up to something. You cheating on me?"

"No, no. I swear. I would never."

"You were with another guy when I met you. How can I trust anything you say?"

My mouth drops open, and with wide eyes I look up at him.

Jon pulls me up to him and grinds his hips against mine. "You used to always be so hot for it. Now you're just a frigid bitch to me. Is that why? Are you getting it somewhere else? One of those fancy doctors you working with bending you over in the back room?" he spits in my ear.

I'm crying now, putting my hands on his shoulders in an attempt to push myself away from him. "No, no."

Shaking his head at me, he mumbles, "You better not be." before turning and leaving me there, reeling.

I start shaking so badly my legs collapse, and I fall to the floor beside the bed. Where did that come from, I wonder, trying to understand. It had been months since Jon had touched me, and he had never touched me like that. Did he just accuse me of cheating on him?

With one of the doctors I worked with? He had taken my gesture of making something for him as an admission of guilt. I have no idea how he could even think that of me. Jon knows where I am at practically every moment of the day. It was him, not me, that would take off with no word as to where he was going or when he would be back. Sometimes, I wish he wouldn't come back.

I disregard that thought as soon as it passes through my mind. I would always want Jon with me, the old Jon, the Jon I fell in love with. I just have to figure out what to do to get him back. I know he is hurting and angry because he is out of work. Maybe if I helped him find a job. I am just scared the help would offend him, but things were so much better when he had a job.

When Jon was still working we had our own little morning routine. When our alarm went off, I would jump in the shower while Jon went to the kitchen to start a half pot of coffee and then climbed back into bed and sleep until I was done in the shower. After my shower I would walk, still in a towel, over to his side of the bed and kiss his cheek, my wet hair falling all around his face.

Jon would always pull me down into his arms and kiss or tickle me until I was gasping for air before getting up with a grin to take his shower. I would get dressed and pour each of us a cup of coffee. I took mine with milk and sugar, and Jon took his with just milk. Jon would shave after his shower, and I would bring him his cup of coffee and chat with him while he shaved.

After our coffee, we would brush our teeth, I would throw on some make up, and we would walk out to our cars together, kissing once more before going in our opposite directions. I used to keep a box of breakfast bars in my car and would eat one on the way to work each morning. The office building Jon worked in had a cafeteria that he would get a muffin or bagel from each morning.

When Jon was first laid off, still actively seeking a new job and going on interviews, he kept the same morning schedule, even when he started collecting unemployment. It wasn't until much later that he started sleeping in. Jon had not said anything to me about it and one morning, when I asked him if he had made coffee, he snapped, telling me to make my own.

I made a pot the next day. After my shower, I came over to kiss him on the cheek, and he cussed at me. Told me to "fucking leave him alone." I wasn't opposed to cussing. I did it myself. Guy cuts me off in traffic: asshole. I drop something on my foot: shit. There was a difference between being okay with cussing and being okay with being cussed at.

When it happened, I said nothing, letting myself stew on it all day. When I came home that evening, I told Jon how much it bothered me and to not do it again. His reaction at the time surprised me. Suddenly, I was the one actually at fault in the scenario because, if I had thought about it, by waking him up when he had no job.

What I was truly doing was rubbing it in his face that he had nowhere to go that day while I did. I could see his point and said as much but went on to try and explain that he still should not have cursed at me. It was disrespectful. Jon would not budge his argument that what I had done was worse and that it somehow justified him. The argument was going nowhere so I dropped the subject.

I never went to wake him up again. Over the days that had passed since that argument, I also stopped drinking coffee in the morning because the smell woke him up. I stopped getting dressed in our bedroom because the noise woke him up. Doing anything I could to not accidentally wake him up, like waiting in my car while it warmed up. If the weekends were a judge, Jon didn't wake up in the morning until after ten.

I was fine with this if he was still trying to get another job. In the beginning when I got home from work, Jon would excitedly tell me about all of the places he had applied. When that stopped, I made the mistake of asking him one day.

Jon railed at me, asking me if I thought he just laid around on his ass all day and did nothing. Did I comprehend how tight and difficult the job market currently was? I must have thought so very little of him to assume all of these horrible things of him.

I had tried to explain I thought none of those things, and of course I knew the job market was tight and was only asking a question. It seemed anything I said after that was being twisted around as though I was making a cruel attack on him. I began to doubt myself, wondering if I was so awful and if he would leave me.

That thought horrified me. I loved Jon so much, and we had been through so much together. What I wanted more than anything else was to just go back to how we were when we were happy. I knew that if Jon had a job again things would be better. I just didn't know how to convince him to look for one without seeming pushy or judgmental.

Suddenly, I have a wonderful idea. What if I begin applying to places for him? That way he'd be happy when he got an interview and never even know to be upset if he didn't get called back. At my office we get the daily paper. I could check the wanted ads on my lunch breaks.

Having a plan makes me feel better, I just don't know what to do about the rest of this weekend. I know I should put away the clothes but what after that? Should I stay in the bedroom, away from him? I end up not having to find out. As I am hanging up the last of his shirts I hear the front door shut. Peering through the cracked bedroom door down the hall to the front room, I can see my keys are gone. Jon has gone somewhere.

It's starting to annoy me that he keeps taking my car

without even asking, and I am curious about where he is going or what he is doing. His comments about me cheating on him seemed so outlandish at the time. Could Jon have just been feeling guilt over something he was doing himself?

I spend the rest of the day nervously waiting for Jon to come home. I go back and forth between being concerned over him to wondering where he is. I also tidy up the best I can. If Jon came home, he would be able to see that I had been cleaning and not just lying about. I hope that shows him how hard I am willing to work to make our home a nice place, comfortable for the two of us.

I believe more than anything else that this is only temporary. I have such a perfect picture of what was once in my head that I would do anything to make it reality again. Before I go to bed I pray. I have never been overly religious. I was raised Catholic but don't attend mass anymore. I do believe that there is something out there, some being that possibly had the power to make things better.

I never pray in front of Jon. He would want to know what I'm praying about and would most likely be angry if I told him. My prayers this evening revolve around finding Jon a new job and the hope that he will not be angry when he finds out about it. He is so touchy these days, I am nervous he would consider it a slight. At this point, anything is better than how we are currently living.

I go to sleep. At some point during the night, Jon comes home. It does not wake me this time. I am almost surprised when I see him asleep in our bed the next morning. Saturday had been a stressful day. That could account for why I had slept so soundly.

I ease out of bed and quietly walk into the front room and make myself a piece of toast and eat a yogurt. I am cleaning my plate when Jon walks out of our room. He comes behind me, pushing himself up against me, his hands on my hips. I go still, hands still in the sink. He leans down to kiss my neck. I am too nervous to react. I don't want him to stop. Jon turns me to face him. I stand with my arms out in front of me, dripping water onto the floor. Jon's hands are on my neck as he kisses me. I kiss him back, happy to be in his arms once again.

He makes love to me that morning, playfully pulling me back to our bedroom. It has been at least a month since he had shown any interest. That last time I had initiated it, Jon seemed almost distracted the whole time, avoiding my kisses and leaving the bed once he was finished.

This time is like old times. Jon kissing me and murmuring silly, sexy things to me. I feel as though my prayers are being answered, as though it is a sign that whatever was broken with us can be fixed. I spend most of Sunday in his arms, blissfully happy. He isn't cold or distant. He is charming and loving.

I blush just looking at him.

His eyes flick to mine. "Yes?"

"It's silly" I feel my cheeks redden even more.

His face breaks into an easy smile, my favorite smile, the one that seems to make me weak in the knees. "Grace, your face is bright red. What's got you blushing?"

I cover my face with a sofa cushion and he plops down next to me, pulling me into his lap. His lips are on my neck, my arms linked around his shoulders.

"I just love you so much." I whisper.

He kisses my cheek. "I do too."

Jon makes dinner that night, flirting with me as he cuts up carrots to steam.

He puts on some music and when the food does not need tending pulls me off the sofa and dances me around the room. After dinner, he makes love to me again. I fall asleep in his arms as he absentmindedly plays with my hair, my body tucked into the crook of his arm. It is the best day.

When my alarm goes off Monday morning, I roll over to him and kiss him. Jon is still mainly asleep and doesn't react. I smile at him, so certain that we will be able to fix this. I get up to take my shower and come back into the bedroom to get dressed. Normally, I would have put my scrubs in the bathroom the night before, but I was distracted and having so much fun with Jon I had forgotten.

"Do you have to make so much fucking noise?"

I am pulling my shirt over my head when Jon says that. Of course, how stupid of me. "I'm so sorry. You won't hear another sound," I whisper as I grab my bottoms and tip toe back to the bathroom.

I begin berating myself for doing something that I knew would annoy Jon. I had stupidly thought that maybe since things seemed like before that I could, well act like I had as well. It was silly of me to assume that. Now all I do is worry that maybe my actions will cause Jon to revert. That is the last thing I want. I take extra care to be as quiet as possible. I gently close the door behind me as I leave to go sit in my car while it warms up.

Walking up to it, I cannot miss the new, decent-sized dent by the front driver's side tire. I close my eyes and take a deep breath. My fingers lightly trace the edge of the indention, bumpy and misshapen in relation to the smooth exterior surrounding it. Was this what yesterday had been all about? Did I get sympathy sex because Jon dented my car?

The dent is on the side of the tire well away from the door. I get in and start the heat and defrosters. As the car warms up I wonder if he had been in an accident with another car or just randomly hit something. If it was with another car could I be sued for damages? Did he hit something or was he hit by something? Part of me wants to march right up those stairs and demand answers from him, while another part of me is scared of his reaction.

Once my car warms up I begin my drive into work, paying special attention in case it seems to handle funny. I'm in luck because it's driving okay. As I cross the river, I think about my parents. My mother would have known what to do with Jon, or my father would have beat him up, not badly, just enough to scare him.

I feel overwhelmed and weepy, wishing they were still alive. I had been close with my mom. We talked more than any of my friends and their moms. I could pick up the phone and tell her anything. My mom was good at not judging and seemed to always have the best advice.

I wish I could have called her right then. I don't want to talk to any of my coworkers about Jon. It was embarrassing. Between moving to the new apartment and being so busy with Jon, I had lost contact with my girlfriends from my single days. Would they even care or understand? Would they just want me to give up on Jon and call it quits? No one would be able to understand how good we had been together and how desperately I wanted that Jon back. Right now, though, what I wanted most of all was someone that I could talk to.

When I get to work, I take care to park the car in a way that the damage could not be seen by my coworkers. I switch my computer on and go to put my lunch in the fridge. Nikita is starting her computer and chatting animatedly about what she had done over the weekend, asking if I had done anything fun. I am checking the appointment log, thinking to myself that it is going to be a busy day, and didn't hear Nikita the first time.

"Did you do anything fun over the weekend?" Nikita repeated herself.

"Oh, no, not really. Laundry."

Nikita's expression makes it clear she thinks that is a waste of a weekend. I listen quietly, nodding at all of the right moments as Nikita continues to gush about her weekend. I feel a little jealous, partly wishing I could go out bar hopping with a group of girls.

Almost as though Nikita is reading my mind, she gives me an open invitation to go out with her sometime. It's sweet, but as I look at Nikita, with all of her enthusiasm for life I just cannot relate to her. I thank her and go back to getting set up for the day.

It's wintertime in Cleveland. To say we are busy with sick appointments is an understatement. I am on my feet most of the day and grateful for the distraction from Jon. At lunch, after bathing in hand sanitizer, I eat my sandwich and comb the want ads for anything Jon could be qualified for. There are some promising ads I circle.

I brought a copy of Jon's most recent resume with me to work and fax it off before clocking back in. I spend the afternoon avoiding sneezes and coughs, silently admonishing some patients to cover their mouths. There seems to be a bug going around. I suck on a vitamin C drop and hope it skips me. Getting sick is the occupational hazard of working in a doctor's office.

In general, I am somewhat impervious to most of the bugs that go around and am very good about getting a flu shot every year, considering they're an employment perk of where I work. Still, a bug knocks me on my ass every couple of years, and I am due for one. Just the thought of it make me squirt an extra dollop of sanitizer onto my hands. Once the last patient is checked out, I sit down to catch my breath.

It doesn't last long. I still have to tidy up the waiting room. My plan is to avoid getting sick, so I put on a pair of gloves before I stack and straighten all of the magazines in the waiting room. Considering the very visible waste basket in the waiting room, I am not pleased to find candy wrappers and used tissues on one of the tables.

Nikita and I walk out together. I am dreading going home, I know I have to bring up the dent but am not sure how to do it. If I ignore it I wonder if Jon will stay as sweet as he had been to me the day before. It's not like being annoyed with him will change the fact that there is a dent. What if he had been at home all day sick with worry about how I would react?

On the drive home I decide not to bring up the dent and see if Jon will. I can picture walking in the door to Jon making something in the kitchen. He would walk over to help me take off my coat and kiss me, asking how my day was. We would have dinner together, and it would be the first step to being us again.

If I could just ignore this maybe that would happen, and wouldn't that be worth it in the long run? I was home. I park, take a deep breath, and after collecting my things, make my way up to our apartment. There had been a dreary drizzle of freezing rain most of the day. Expecting slick spots, I slowly make my way up the stairs.

The apartment is dark when I walk in. I flip on the light for the front room and look around. I stop myself from calling out to Jon in case he is sleeping. I hang up my keys and purse, then take off my coat before moving further into the apartment, turning on lights as I go. The door to our bedroom is cracked. I peer inside, expecting to see Jon lying in our bed. He isn't. Where is he? I walk back out to the kitchen to see if maybe he left a note before getting my cell phone from my purse to check for a text. Nothing.

I think about texting him to ask where he is, but the last time I had done that he had become so annoyed. He had implied that my asking where he was, was an accusation. It didn't matter that I tried to explain I only wanted to find out if I should be cooking for two or just myself. Jon wasn't always this defensive. Only in the last year. In the past he had been so confident and so sure of our bond. He also had an uncanny way of knowing what I was thinking of asking before I did. He seems to have lost that.

I think back to the two resumes I had faxed off for him that day with a wish in my heart that something good would come of it. I make myself a sandwich and pull out a photo album from when we first started dating. It's a black padded album with slots for two pictures and a comment on each page, with a spot for one photo on the cover. I trace Jon's handsome profile on the cover picture. It's a shot of us looking at each other. I laugh, looking at our sappy expressions. My laugh becomes a choked sob at the thought of how different we are today. Taking a napkin to stem the flow of tears, I close my eyes, pushing the album away.

Today is not a good day to look at it, maybe tomorrow. Getting up to wash my plate, I feel flushed. Raising the back of my hand to my forehead, I grimace at how warm it feels. I wash my plate, take some aspirin, and then suck on a vitamin C drop. I am not going to get sick. There are few things I can control right now, but I am convinced getting sick is one of them. Changing into my pajamas, I am sure that a good night's sleep will kick whatever funk may be lurking. Still hot, I shove most of the comforter towards Jon's side of the bed.

For the most part, I sleep well with the exception of freezing at some points and then feeling too warm. When I wake and see that Jon is still not home, I'm relieved because I am certain he would have been annoyed that I tossed and turned all night. That feeling is short-lived and replaced by a combination of concern at where he is to annoyance at how inconsiderate it is of him. Those feelings are pushed aside as I hurry to get ready for work. While I do not feel one hundred percent, I no longer feel feverish. Instead, I feel foggy, as though there is a hum in my ears and my limbs have fallen asleep. But I can function.

Since Jon is not home, there's no point sitting in a cold car as it warms up. I carefully hurry down the stairs to start my car and then quickly back up the stairs, sliding for a nerve-wrecking moment near the top. Once inside, I brush my teeth, gather my things, and after peeking to see the front window is now clear, make my way back down the stairs. Crossing the river, I send out a little wish to my parents to watch out for Jon.

Whatever energy I had managed to find to drag myself to work doesn't last long, My fog descends once again, and I struggle through my day. At lunch, instead of checking the want ads for Jon, I lay my head on the table in the break room and take a catnap, waking with an imprint of my watchband on my cheek. Nikita encourages me to go home early to get more rest, but I wave her off. In my eyes, there is no point, since it is now after lunch. There are only four more hours to go. I can do that in my sleep.

With only the occasional head bob, I finish my shift. When I get into my car, I immediately switch the stereo to a metal station, hopeful the screaming will keep me conscious for the ride home. Visions of a bowl of chicken noodle soup carry me home. After parking, I notice that the front light is on. I am too tired to contemplate whether

I am happy or not to know that Jon is home. I take my time up the stairs and hardly notice or care that Jon seems tense when I walk in. I drop my things by the door and shuffle to the kitchen. Jon looks at me in confusion, and I admit that I do not feel good.

Taking a pan out to heat a can of soup, I struggle to keep my mouth from hanging open when Jon casually asks if I can make him some soup as well. Turning quickly so Jon will not see the pained look on my face, I say, "Sure."

"And some toast?"

I nod. Really, I am already making myself a bowl. It isn't any bother to add another can to the pot and pop another slice of toast in the toaster. It's no more work than what I have already intended to do, and even though I tell myself this, it does not hurt any less that he had not offered to make it himself since he knows I am not feeling well. I tuck that feeling way deep inside where I can ignore it because thinking about it just makes me feel worse.

I serve Jon and myself once the soup is hot. Jon finishes eating before I do and leaves his plate and bowl in the sink for me. I wash them along with my plate and bowl once I finish eating, tucking how that makes me feel inside as well. I could have said something, but really, considering I just want to go to sleep, how will it accomplish anything?

At best, Jon would apologize after we talked it out and say he would be more considerate in the future, and at worst, somehow it would all turn into my fault, and I would end up feeling worse than I already did. In either scenario, a conversation will be needed, and honestly I do not want to talk to Jon, although I tell myself it's because I'm tired and just want to go to sleep.

Jon doesn't seem to mind that I go to sleep early. I am so exhausted I don't even feel the movement of him climbing into bed at some point overnight. When my alarm clock goes off the next day, and I feel no improvement from the night's rest, I know taking a sick day is my only option. I send a text to the office manager and to Nikita to let them know I'll be out.

Nikita replies almost instantly, telling me that she hopes I feel better. I turn the ringer off and turn over to go back to sleep. I wake again when Jon begins rustling. Jon snuggles up next to me, pressing himself against me. I feel like crap and turn away from him in an attempt to avoid his amorous attention.

"What's your problem?" he asks angrily.

"I just don't feel good." I mumble.

"I don't know why I even bother," Jon huffs as he gets out of bed and storms out of the room.

I lie still as can be, almost frozen by his words. Part of me wants to call him back and do whatever he wants to make him happy. Another part wonders why it is so wrong to not feel good and how Jon can be annoyed at me for it. I feel a sense of shame inside, thinking that there must be something wrong with me that would make Jon act so cold. I feel an overwhelming sense of inadequacy until my exhaustion takes over, and I fall asleep.

I wake up again maybe three hours later to the sound of noise coming from the front room. Putting on my robe, I slowly make my way out of the bedroom to see what all of the noise is. The movement makes me feel weak. I have yet to eat or drink anything and am most likely dehydrated. The sound of gunfire from the television is a roar as I approach the front room. When I get there, I see Jon and a neighbor have set up a video game system in the living room and are playing what looks like a war game.

Our neighbor, a young guy who lives on the first floor sees me walk in. "Oh man, did we wake you?"

I look at Jon, my brows furrowed. I just do not understand what this guy is doing in our apartment. I know none of the video game stuff is ours. Jon had sold everything he had when he was trying to figure out a way to keep his car. Jon shrugs at me and looks back at the TV. Our neighbor sees my confusion and offers to leave.

I wave him off and walk over to the kitchen to get some crackers and a glass of water before returning to bed. With the door closed and the small TV in our room on, I can't hear the noise from the front room anymore. I nibble on my crackers and sip my water, trying my best to finish them before I fall back asleep.

It's dark outside when I wake again, and the apartment is quiet. My appetite has improved so I make my way to the kitchen to make something. The front room is dark, and there is no sign of Jon. I glance over to the pile of my things on the floor by the door and see that my keys are also gone. He had taken my car again.

We had never discussed the dent, and now he is gone again. I wonder how Jon would react if I told him I did not want him using my car unless he checked with me first. I do not think he would react well to that, but it bothers me so much that he keeps taking it without asking.

Exhausted from the activity, I retreat back to our room to sleep. When my alarm clock goes off the next morning, I still feel rough but well enough to go to work. I always hate calling in sick and am already feeling guilty for missing the previous day. When I go to shower I realize Jon is not in bed. I rush into the front room to see if maybe he's sleeping on the sofa. He isn't.

Opening the door to our apartment, I ignore the cold blast of air and rush to the landing to see if my car is in its spot. It's not. Even if I had wanted to go to work, I can't. I am too stunned that he had not come home to react immediately. I call my office manager and lie, saying

I am still not feeling well enough to come back and send a text message to Nikita. I get two texts messages back, one from my manager letting me know I can take all the time I need and another from Nikita that is just a frown face.

This is bullshit, and there is no way I can ignore it. This can affect my job and being able to pay our bills. I cannot help but be concerned as well. What if he had been in an accident and is hurt somewhere? Slumping onto our bed, I go back and forth between whether I should call him or not.

Caving, I call him, chewing on my fingernail as it rings and rings and goes to voicemail. In the message I leave him, I try to sound as calm as possible. I let him know I am worried about him and am curious where he is because I need the car to go to work. I hang up, and I pause to reflect on my choice of words. The car. Not that long ago, I had always called it mine.

I lie down with my phone propped up in front of me so I won't miss his call, but it's the front door I hear three hours later instead. I had taken a shower and made myself some breakfast while waiting. I am grateful for being up and dressed when I walk into the front room to see a group of people there. I only recognize the neighbor who had been there the day before. There are six people total, four guys and two girls.

"Shouldn't you be lying down?" Jon says, looking everywhere but at me as a couple of his new friends snicker behind him.

"Can we talk?" I say quietly as I gesture toward our bedroom.

"Yeah, sure. Hey guys, hang out here."

Jon hurries past me and down the hall to our room. I'm still not feeling great so I follow him slowly. He's sitting down on his side of the bed, up against his pillows, legs crossed at his ankles in front of him. He looks very relaxed.

"What did you want to talk about?"

My mouth drops open. Did he really just ask me that? I cock my head to the side and look at him as though I have never seen him before. It's like he's a stranger sitting on my bed. I am rendered momentarily speechless and close the door behind me.

"Jon, where were you?"

"Just hanging out."

"I missed work because you had the car." There it was again, the car.

"I thought you'd still be sick today."

I walk over to sit on my side of the bed. When I sit, Jon gets up and goes to stand by the door. Why did he get up?

"Are you leaving?"

"Yeah. We were going to head over to the thing."

The thing? "Are you taking the car?" The car.

"Yeah. You're just going to be in bed."

"I'm going to work tomorrow so I need the car to be here." The car.

"Yeah, yeah..." and he was out the door.

No apology. No "how are you feeling?" I sit there wondering what those people in my front room had thought of me, wonder if he had even said anything about me. Not one of them had made a move to introduce themselves. I suddenly feel paranoid, like I'm the butt of a joke. Maybe Jon will be home early enough tonight that we will have a chance to talk about it. I decide I'll rest during the day and make a nice dinner for the both of us. If I have the ingredients, I'll even make Jon's favorite: enchiladas.

I spend most of the day stressing out over where Jon is and what he might be doing. He's been taking off so much recently I don't know how I should feel about it. I'm a mixture of emotions and can't choose just one. I feel abandoned, jealous, insecure, hurt, and sad all at the same time. I cannot understand why I feel the need to constantly walk around on eggshells around him while he cannot even bother to be polite to me. How is that fair? At this point, I would be so blown over by any small gesture of affection. Can he see that?

I change my clothes into something slightly nicer than the sweats I've worn all day and make the enchiladas. As I slide them in the oven to cook, I wonder if it had been silly of me to even assume he will be coming home at dinnertime. I check my phone to see if he had maybe sent me a text. He hasn't. While dinner cooks, I second-guess myself, not sure if this had been a good idea. At worst I'll eat alone and pack up the leftovers to take to work as lunch the next day. I turn on the TV to act as a distraction from the thoughts crowding my mind. Watching the news, I learn there is snow in the forecast and dream of someday living someplace warmer.

Jon never shows up. I eat by myself and pack up the leftovers. I leave a note on the fridge that there are leftovers in case Jon is hungry when he gets home. Wanting to be fully rested for work the next day, I head to bed early. When my alarm clock goes off, I'm relieved to see Jon asleep next to me. He must have come home at some point after I went to sleep. Careful not to wake him, I get ready for work. When I go to the kitchen, I see that he hasn't eaten the enchiladas and decide to take them with me for lunch, throwing away the note on the fridge.

As I sit in my car while it warms up, I notice the tank is on E. It had been almost full the last time I had driven it. I'll have to stop on the way in to work to get some gas. It annoys me, but Jon doesn't have any money so it's not like he can buy any gas either way. It would have been nice if he had gotten a couple of bucks from his new friends. I'm worried about filling it up all the way in case he takes the car again. I can't afford to be filling it up all the time. I fill it up halfway and continue on my way to work. Nikita's parking at the same time I'm parking and rushes over to greet me.

"How are you feeling? Oh my gosh, Grace. What happened to your car?"

I grimaced. "I feel better. Thanks. Jon hit something."

"I'm so happy you're feeling better. That sucks about your car. What'd he hit?"

"Not sure. We haven't really talked about it."

"No way. You are so nice. I would have lost it."

We chat as we head into the office. It's Friday, and there are many last-minute sick appointments. It seems like whatever I had is going around big time. At lunch, I look over the want ads, not seeing anything that might be a good fit for Jon. I wonder about the two places I had sent his resume to and if they had contacted him. If they had, Jon had not said anything. After lunch, I dip into my spare change dish to buy a soda. It's been the first day in a while that I had been so active, and I really need some caffeine.

It has been a long day, and I am grateful once the day ended and I can go home. All I want to do is make myself another can of soup and go back to bed. Not feeling as though I am in any danger of falling asleep behind the wheel, I skip the metal station this time. Jon is in the front room when I get home, watching TV.

"What happened to the enchiladas?"

"What?"

He stood. "What happened to the enchiladas?" He enunciates each word.

Oh no, I think. "I took them to work for lunch today. I

didn't know you wanted them. I thought that since you had not eaten them last night that you had not wanted them."

"No. I was actually saving them for lunch for myself today. Just think of how I must have felt when I went to the fridge and found out they were gone."

Couldn't have been worse than the feeling I had when I saw my car was gone the day before, I thought to myself. I don't say it, though. That would only make things worse.

"I can run to the store and get stuff to make some tonight. Would you like that? I'm so sorry. I did not know you wanted them."

"Don't bother. It's already done."

"Well, let me make you something else. What would you like?"

I end up making spaghetti and meatballs per Jon's request. Sure, it's not the soup I wanted, but it's still good and now Jon is less upset. After dinner, I wash the pots and pans and dirty dishes from our meal. Jon returns to his armchair and is watching TV. Once I'm done, I go to bed. The next morning, I am relieved to see Jon asleep again beside me. As I was falling asleep last night, I worried that he might go out again. I quietly get out of bed and make myself a cup of tea and some toast.

After washing my cup and plate, I sit down on the sofa to read. My plans for the day are simple: rest, and maybe later on take a couple loads of laundry down to the Laundromat. I am well into my book when Jon comes out of our bedroom. He nods in my direction before making himself a bowl of cereal. I hold my spot in my book with my hand as I watch him eat. I still think he is so handsome, although recently he looks more tired than he had in the past. If only he could find a job.

"Want something?"

I had zoned off and didn't realize he had noticed me staring at him.

"Oh, I was just thinking."

"About what?"

"It's silly."

"I'm listening."

"I was just thinking how handsome you are." I am not sure why saying that embarrasses me. I used to tell him that all the time.

Jon shakes his head at me, not looking convinced, and goes back to his breakfast. I return to my book. When he finishes eating, Jon sets his bowl and spoon in the sink for me to clean. I rest my book on the arm of the sofa and go to wash them.

For the most part, over the weekend, we steer clear of each other. If Jon is in the front room, I am in the bedroom and vice versa. Lying in the same bed as Jon each night, I am aware of the fact that I have never felt so distant from him. He doesn't talk to me anymore.

It's like living with a stranger. I lie in bed thinking of how I can find intimacy with Jon again. It's hard for me to understand how we have gone from telling each other everything to this. I try not to dwell on thoughts like these. It's too painful to take alone, and since I can no longer confide in Jon, I feel as though I have no one else.

When I interact with coworkers and patients at work on Monday, I feel like a fraud. I smile and laugh when socially appropriate, but there is a hollowness building within me. Sometimes I wonder how everyone around me cannot tell how unhappy I am. Everyone I work with is so busy with their own lives that they don't seem to notice the change in me, or if they do, no one mentions it. That does not help me from feeling isolated. Even Nikita, who always cheers me up, is preoccupied with something that day.

I feel so overwhelmed by my loneliness that I cry most of my drive home. Crossing the river is particularly hard today. I miss my parents and want more than anything else to talk to my mother. Not that I want to say anything. I just want to feel her embrace and hear her voice again. I dry my eyes once I park, hopeful Jon won't notice how red they are.

I'm barely in the door when Jon says, "Were you going to tell me?"

I look to where he is sitting, confused, not sure what he's talking about.

"You didn't think I would figure it out when they contacted me?"

Someone contacted him. Could it be about one of the resumes I sent? "Did you get an interview?"

"So it was you. No, I did not get an interview. What I got was the opportunity to make a complete ass out of myself when they called because I had no idea who they were and why the fuck they were calling me."

"Oh no." This was not good. I close my eyes and set my things down as he continues.

"You didn't think it might help to tell me someone might be calling me? Or did you just want me to sound like a complete idiot on the phone with them?"

"I was only trying to help."

"Sure you were. Can you do me a favor and let me fucking handle it?"

"I just thought—"

"No, you didn't fucking think."

Tears cloud my eyes as I rush to our room and shut the door. Jon is close behind me, though, and pushes the door open. "Don't you ever walk away from me when I am talking to you."

I cover my ears with my hands and look down as I try to block him out. Jon stands over me almost panting with anger. After a few moments, I peer up at where Jon had been standing to find I am now alone. As my heart slowly stops pounding, I pull my legs into my chest and hug them, jerking up at the sound of the front door slamming.

Jon has left, and I am grateful for it. My only fear is about my car not being back in time for me to get to work the next day. It's the first time Jon has left that I can admit I'm not sure if I even want him to come back. I wonder if maybe Jon had been pushing me away on purpose. Maybe he didn't love me anymore but doesn't have anywhere else to go.

I venture out into the kitchen to make a plate of cheese and crackers before retreating to our bedroom. Jon had scared me and somehow I feel safer in the bedroom. I think about locking the door but don't want to upset Jon more than I already have. I feel stupid for even hoping that I could have found Jon a job. I had known deep down that it was something he needed to do on his own. I just could not understand why my trying to help him had made him so angry with me. Was it just that the call had caught him off guard or was it more?

I stiffen when I hear the front door open a couple of hours later. Quickly turning off the light, I pretend to be asleep. I hear Jon walk into our room, and then a few moments later, walk back out. I wonder if I should go to him and try and talk about what had happened that day but don't know what type of mood he's in so think it safer to talk another time. The next morning, after getting ready for work, I write Jon a note. I tell him that I'm sorry about not telling him I sent his resumé places. I had honestly thought if he got a call back he would have been happy. I end the note with I love you.

As I sit in the car while it warms up, I see that I need gas. Again. I stop at a station and have a mild shock when I pull out my wallet and find it empty. I had sixty dollars, and it's gone. Jon took money from me. I sit immobilized as I process this. I lean my head back against the car seat and stare up at the ceiling.

Anger

a strong feeling of displeasure and usually of antagonism
-Merriam Webster

Calm down, calm down. I feel the pulse of my blood pounding all over me. I try to catch my breath. How do people calm down? Count to ten? I count, and that doesn't work. Maybe if I count backwards. Ten, nine, eight, seven, six, five, four, three, two, one…I slowly catch my breath. I'm done with being nice. Now I'm angry. I grab my purse and head into the gas station to use the ATM. I don't plan to take any money out, but I want to check my balance before I try to use my card to pay for gas. I'm relieved when the balance is what I expect. I walk back out to the pump and start fueling up. It's cold out so I wait in my car. To anyone else fueling at that station that morning, I appear to be having a very heated discussion alone. I scream at myself for being so stupid and letting Jon walk all over me these past months. When had I become such a wuss? My parents had raised me to have a backbone and here I was completely failing at it.

I decide to fill up my tank because there is no way I am going to let Jon take it again. As I sit in my car, I wonder how easy it would be to change the PIN number on my card. If Jon had taken money out of my wallet, what would stop him from trying to use my card at an ATM? Once my tank is full, I continue on to work. As I drive, I think about sending Jon a text to let him know I know what he did and to finally confront him about the dent. I'm angry I let that go. I finally realize I'm angry about a lot of things. This is just the final straw.

One thing I learn about anger is how energizing it feels. Adrenaline is pumping me up, and it bleeds into my driving. A car rudely, with no signal indication, cuts me off before a red light. I take deep breaths and talk myself out of ramming the asshole driving the Ford. Instead, I coldly glare at the driver in front of me. I turn right as the other driver continues straight, and after I park, I laugh out loud when I see the same driver pull into my parking lot from a different entrance.

"Serves you right," I mumble. "You drove like an asshole, and I still beat you. Ha!"

That small victory is enough to cheer me up and make me laugh, calming me a bit. I'm setting up the sign-in sheet when Nikita walks in.

"Good morning," I greet her happily.

Nikita looks at me for a beat. "You seem to be chipper this morning. What's going on?"

"I have been in a bit of a funk, haven't I?"

"A bit…" Nikita deadpans, which makes me laugh.

"Yes, well, I'm done with that."

"I'm happy to hear that."

Nikita asks me a couple of times what has changed or what has been bothering me. I avoid the questions, not wanting to get that personal at work and tell Nikita that with the holidays and being sick I have just been missing my parents more. This isn't completely untrue. It just doesn't include the fact that I had decided I'm not going to let Jon walk all over me anymore. If Jon can't accept some responsibility and start pulling his own weight, I'm done.

I'm still young, and while I currently do everything in my power to downplay my looks, I know I'm pretty. If Jon can't handle being civil to me, I'm sure someone else will. Not that I want that, because even though I'm furious with Jon, I still love him and am hopeful that we can get past this. If we can't get past it, I know that I won't be happy walking on eggshells the rest of my life. I would rather die alone than accept the way Jon makes me feel any longer. Things are going to change. How much, depends on Jon.

Jon had never really seen me angry. With the exception of the last year, he had never given me a reason to be really angry. I spend most of the day wondering why I had not stood up to him from the start. That first morning he had yelled at me for waking him up, I should have gotten right in his face and screamed back. I think of the story of Ferdinand The Bull. I am a Taurus, born the end of April. I had always related to Ferdinand because it did take a lot to make me angry. Jon will get his first taste tonight.

I watch the clock more than normal, I used to lament going home but, now I cannot wait. In my mind I think of everything I have not said over the past year. When it's time to go, I practically fly to my car. Crossing the river, I ask my parents to give me strength. I focus all of my attention on just how angry I am, not wanting to lose any momentum. After parking I race up the stairs. They're slick as usual so after almost tumbling down them. I take a moment to relax and continue up them with more care.

After turning the lock, I fling open the door, making Jon jump as he sits in his armchair.

"What the hell?" he sputters.

"Yes! What the hell!"

Jon looks at me like I have grown two heads and doesn't say anything.

I slam the door shut and drop my things next to it. I'm pleased that he's still sitting, and I'm standing. It makes me feel bigger than him. I also feel like I need to move around.

"What happened to the sixty dollars that was in my wallet, Jon?"

"That's what all of this is about?"

"Oh, I haven't even started. Do you admit it? Did you take money out of my wallet?"

Jon doesn't say anything, but his whole body is tense, and his fingers are flexing open and shut on the arms of the chair.

"Since you have nothing to say, I can only assume that, yes, you did take it."

Jon stands up now. "So you're throwing it in my face that you have money, and I don't?

Is that what this is?"

I was not having it. "Don't even go there. This is about you taking money without asking.

That's a big difference, because face it, we have bills to pay that I have to budget for."

"So I'm like a child getting an allowance. You want to control me."

"You have got to be freaking kidding me. I'm asking for two adults to have a conversation."

"Whatever." Jon makes to go pick up the car keys, but I grab them first and hold them behind my back. "Not going to happen. Let me be crystal clear about this. From this moment on, the only time you will be driving *my* car is when I say so."

"Is that so?"

"I'm done."

"You're done? What the fuck does that mean?"

"I can't do this anymore."

"Can't do what? Us? That's real fucking nice after everything we've been through."

"You don't even act like you like me. Do you even want to be here?"

"Can you even understand the amount of stress I'm under?"

"The stress you're under? The stress *you're under*? What do you *do* all day? When was the last time you applied anywhere? I got my head bit off because I sent your resume someplace."

"I was only mad because you didn't tell me about it."

"And how much sense does that make? To get mad at someone for trying to help you?"

"I don't have to listen to this." Jon grabs his coat and keys then walks out the door.

I stand there panting, my chest rising and falling as I breathe out my nose. Finally, speaking up for myself feels so liberating. So why do I feel like crying? The whole exchange had just been so overwhelmingly emotional. For a moment I pity him, out there in the cold. That feeling lasts only long enough for me to remind myself that I have to sit out there in the cold every morning while my car warms up. There is no way I will ever do that again. In fact, I have every intention of being as loud as humanly possible the next morning.

What if he doesn't come back? I sit at our small table and wonder how I'll feel if that happens. As angry as I am, I do still love him. It's clear that I have been denying that there was anything wrong with his behavior for a long time. What scares me about the whole situation is it's out of my hands to a certain extent. It's Jon who needs to change, not me. Not that I'm innocent. I had knowingly enabled Jon. I thought it would help, but it's clear that it hasn't.

On the off chance Jon will try and take my wallet or keys, I hide them in a kitchen cabinet where I store my mother's old Kitchenaid mixer. My stomach is too messed up to eat anything. I go back and forth between relief in blowing up to being nervous that I may have gone too far. The adrenaline wears off, and I go to sleep. At some point overnight, I hear Jon come home and climb into bed. When my alarm clock goes off the next morning, I get ready for work. I'm not being loud on purpose, but I'm also not trying to be very quiet either. Part of me stays coiled like a cobra, waiting to strike, willing Jon to say something. He doesn't.

It almost feels like a missed opportunity to release more of my pent up aggression on him. There is so much that remains unsaid. Most importantly, him saying he's sorry. Retrieving my keys and wallet from the cabinet, I hurry down the stairs to warm up my car. I loudly come back into the apartment. Jon is either still asleep or pretending to be. If he keeps taking off, we will never fix what's wrong, and our conversation from last night is not over.

I'm irritable on my drive in. It's like every person on the road is driving like an idiot. I'm tired of it, tired of everything. I am tired of the cars that pull out even though they see me coming. How do they know I will slow down? What if I don't slow down? I hate the cars that drive five miles under the speed limit until you try to pass them. I hate the cars that don't use their turn signals. What am I? Psychic?

I have always been easygoing and mild-mannered, but it's as though a switch of some sort has been flipped. I have no patience for anyone around me, starting with Jon and now including my co-workers and the patients. I count to ten to control myself more that day than I ever have in my life. By the end of the day, it's no longer working, and I snap at Nikita for something. The injured look on her face makes me feel awful so I immediately apologize. I have to get a hold of myself. Instead of counting to ten, I start counting backwards from one hundred.

I feel the pressure of not having to deal with anyone evaporate the second I am in my car. Just like that morning, it seems like the other commuters are purposely trying to aggravate me. I consider road raging on the Lexus that isn't paying attention and honk my horn to let him know the light has changed to green. Counting from one hundred isn't working either. By the time I pull into my parking spot, my body is humming with energy. Great time to finish my conversation with Jon. I am actually looking forward to laying into him. Jon is in the kitchen making dinner when I walk in, not in his beloved armchair.

"Hello, Jon."

"How was your day?"

"Just great," I huff sarcastically.

"Ahhh..."

"We need to talk."

"I know."

He knows? I breathe in and out of my nose, short bursts of air that almost feel heated. It's nice that he knows and just took off while we were mid conversation yesterday. Is he just going to do the same thing today?

Jon watches, he hesitates "Grace?"

Not able to hold myself together, I scream. "I am so mad right now!"

"Why? Did something happen?"

Wrong question, mister. "I've been holding everything in for so long about what you have been doing and how you have been making me feel and how ashamed I am at myself that I never said anything. I just let you. I let you put me down, and I felt bad when I annoyed you, and I made myself feel like it was me, like I was the problem. Like if I did something you would be nice again. I did everything I could think of just for you to be nice to me. How sad is that? How pathetic am I? And what did you do? You take my car and go God knows where with God knows who and you dent it. You dented my car! How did that happen? Were you ever going to say anything to me?"

Jon stares at me open mouthed, his wooden spoon frozen midair since he had been about to stir something on the stovetop. I put my hand on the back of one of the chairs of our small table to hold myself up. I feel short of breath, as though I had spoken that entire stream of words without stopping to breathe. I drop my head to look at the ground while my heart stops thumping. After a couple moments, I look back up at Jon who still looks dumbstruck.

And there is that feeling again, anger. "Say something!"

"I…I…I…"

"You what?"

"God, Grace. Calm down—"

I cut him off, bringing up the hand that had been clenching the back of the chair to point at him. "Don't tell me to calm down. I am so fucking sick of your shit."

I was never much of a cusser. In fact, that's part of the reason it really bothers me when Jon cusses at me. Jon looks dazed as he raises both hands, palms out. I lower my hand and pace randomly around our front room. I want to hit something. I come close to punching the wall but do not want to hurt my hand or have to explain any damage to the landlord. Jon takes whatever he is cooking off the stove and follows me into the front room. I look out the window to the courtyard below. Jon is standing a few feet to my side.

Keeping my body facing the window, I look at him out of the corner of my eyes. "You talk."

Jon sits in his armchair. He drops his head into his hands and runs his fingers through his hair, shaking his head and nervously tapping one foot. He looks over at me a couple of times, trying to meet my gaze, but I keep my eyes on a small bird sitting on the back of a bench. While I wait for Jon to speak, I wonder how the little bird is faring out in the cold. Part of me wants to rush outside to save it. Instead, I watch as it flies somewhere out of sight. Jon still hasn't said anything so I clear my throat as I wait for him to get to it.

He sighs before straightening back up. "I'll admit I've made some mistakes."

I mouth the word "some."

"I just am under so much stress, and yes, I may not have handled it well."

I mouth the word "may."

"I just don't know how to deal with this and…"

He seems to have lost his train of thought at that point so I turn, crossing my arms over my chest. "You may have made some mistakes? Do you really feel that way? Please, by all means, tell me what you have been doing otherwise, and I'd still really love to hear what happened to my car."

Jon stands, moving closer to me and tells me that the night the dent happened he had been over at someone's house. I don't recognize the name. Another person there that night had backed into my car as they were leaving. Since the damage had been minimal, he had told the girl not to worry about it. Girl, I thought. Interesting.

"It was really thoughtful of you to not be worried

about the dent in *my* car that I'm going to have to pay money for at some point to get fixed."

"If it's that big of a deal I'll pay to have it fixed—" he begins.

I have to stop him, incredulous. "With what money, Jon?"

He shrugs. Thought so. As he stands there, I look at him as if it's for the first time. He seems almost smaller, with his shoulders pulled inward. I am repulsed. I sink down onto the sofa and turn away from him. Jon stays where he is, as if waiting for me to tell him what to do next. All I can think is: do I still love him? This is unexpected. Needing space from Jon, I tell him I'm not hungry and just need to lie down. I avoid touching him as I squeeze past him and go to our room.

I place my car keys and purse in an empty shoebox on the floor of the closet, still not trusting Jon. Then I change into pajamas and stretch out on our bed. I don't mean to fall asleep but am so drained from the day that I have little choice. An hour before my alarm normally goes off, I wake up starving. I feel guilty for a moment when I see the leftovers from the meal Jon had made the night before in the fridge. Then I remember the cinnamon rolls I had made, and the mess I had to clean up. Yep, no longer feeling guilty.

I make myself scrambled eggs and toast, washing them down with milk. Then I go back into our room to turn off my alarm before getting ready for work like normal. This morning, I put on make-up. Not much, just concealer under my eyes and mascara. I also braid my hair instead of pulling it back into my usual tight bun. I want to feel good about myself again. It amazes me how now, even though I am no longer taking extreme care to be quiet, that Jon has not said one word. All of those times he had railed at me in the past seem to be a lie now.

On my drive into work, I spend more time thinking about Jon's behavior over the last year. It's almost clear to me that he was trying to make me feel bad about myself. Did it have something to do with control? I just cannot understand the thought process behind doing that to someone you loved. For so long I had absolved Jon of any responsibility in my unhappiness. Now I wonder if he is the main cause of it.

At work, I do my best to remain calm with everyone I work with. It's easier than the day before even though there are some close moments where I think about snapping. Once is at lunch. I'm reading a book as I sit in the break room. Two of the nurses who work in my office hover in the doorway and gossip. Can't they see I am on break? And reading? How inconsiderate. The counting backwards by ones is not working so I start counting backwards, this time by sevens. One hundred, ninety-three, eighty-six, seventy-eight, no, nine, seventy-two…

This way, I avoid having any reasons to talk to human resources. I need this job and am not going to let my bad mood affect it. I have never been this angry for this long, and I'm not certain how to make the feeling go away. I assumed laying into Jon would have worked, but if anything, now that I've unleashed on him a couple times, it's made it harder not to do that every time I'm around him. There is no way I want to emulate the way he has treated me so I do my best to keep most of my possible outbursts to myself.

I'm not successful all of the time. One weekend morning, after Jon finishes his breakfast, he puts the plate and silverware in the sink without washing them. I am sitting on the sofa watching TV when I see him do this and explode. I ask if he assumed that I am his maid and that he had another thing coming if he actually thinks I will clean up after him ever again. In fact, I go on that he should be cleaning up after me as a way to pull his own weight. Once he is done with his dishes, he can go ahead and take care of the laundry. Downstairs, of course. I still do not trust Jon with my car keys.

Even though there is an improvement in our relationship, it seems false. When I get home from work, Jon tells me about all of the places he applied. I never check, but I always wonder if he is lying, or at the least exaggerating. A few times, Jon attempts to initiate intimacy between us. I kiss him but nothing more. I cannot get that image of him in our front room with his shoulders shrugged inward out of my mind. It repulsed me then and still does now. Jon does not press me, though, which I am grateful for and concerned about all at the same time.

I'm still angry. I have counted backwards by sevens so many times I now have the numbers memorized and need to start using a different number: eleven. I become hyper aware of wherever Jon is in relation to me in our apartment. If we are both in the front room watching TV, I can feel myself becoming annoyed at the way he is breathing. Why does he have to breathe so loudly? Is he congested? God, that noise! Why doesn't he just blow his nose? And the way he walks around the apartment. Does he have to walk on his heels? Yet, if he walks quietly, I get equally annoyed, wondering if he's doing it on purpose to sneak up on me.

While Jon is no longer snapping at me, I feel no renewed affection for him. I no longer feel like my head will be bitten off out of nowhere but we do not feel like a couple either. We still sleep in the same bed, but we go to sleep at different times, so we aren't ever both in bed and awake at the same time. Even around the apartment we seem to gravitate away from each other. I wonder if the only reason Jon is even still there is because he has nowhere else to go. That's not true, though. He could always move back home or since Jon has always been everyone's best friend he probably has plenty of people that would let him stay with them. What is keeping him here? Is it me?

I am not sure if I love him anymore. I am also sure that we will never go back to what we were. Too much has happened since then. Depending on my mood, I consider asking him to leave, but the idea of being all alone scares me. We have been together for over three years, and most of that had been good. I drive back and forth from work trying to decide what to do over and over again. I imagine the freedom of no longer supporting Jon, of being single again. What stops me is basically how unconfrontational I am. Those blow-ups with Jon had been nurtured within me for a year.

I had finally admitted I was angry and wasn't going to allow Jon to kick me around anymore. Considering how long it finally took me to stand up for myself, how long will it take me to build up the courage to ask him to leave? We basically ignore the holidays this year. No decorations, no parties, no gifts. I am thrilled when it's all over. It's pointless to pretend to be happy. But if I'm not going to leave Jon, this will be my new life. I don't want to spend the rest of my days like this but am hesitant about changing anything. I keep most of what I am feeling inside. Some days I feel really nostalgic, reminiscing over happier days. This feeling usually goes one of two ways; sadness over what we have lost and anger that we allowed it to happen in the first place.

It's so strange to look at Jon when I think about the

days I was so madly in love with him. I still remember so vividly how just the sight of him could make my heart beat wildly in my chest. It is so different now when I look at him. Jon is softer around the waist. Sitting around the apartment did that to him. He never smiles anymore, and his eyes, which had once been so captivating, are dull now. Sometimes I try to imagine the last year from his perspective. I can just never understand why if he had been hurting emotionally instead of coming to me for help he had chosen to instead intimidate me.

It's difficult for me to feel sympathetic towards him when his cruel actions and indifference are still so fresh in my mind. I cannot imagine him touching me romantically again. One day we are both in the kitchen at the same time, and his hand accidentally almost brushes against mine. I jerk my hand back and clutch it to my chest as though the contact had burned me. I do not feel sorrow when I see his wounded reaction. He made me this way. Jon keeps a careful distance after that.

Jon applies for jobs with renewed vigor. I had been certain for so long that he would never find something that it comes as a shock to me when he does. The pay is much less than the job he had lost, but in this economy, he considers himself lucky to have gotten it at all. He works in a warehouse stocking long haul trucks for delivery. This job is very different from the white collar jobs he is used to. The perks are that it's located on a bus line so it doesn't matter that he doesn't have a car, and he only really needs to buy a pair of sturdy steel-toed boots. The other clothes he has are fine.

Our morning routine ends up being similar to what it was in the past. Instead of walking over to kiss him in the morning to let him know the shower is free, I just shout it. Jon breaks out the coffee machine for a couple of cups in the morning. Somehow I can't really drink it anymore, I can't go back to how we were and don't know if I want to start it again. Since it's still very cold in the morning, I drive Jon to the bus stop near our building. As he's getting out of my car one morning, Jon pauses as if he is going to tell me something but then just shakes his head and closes the door. I wonder what he was about to say.

The heavy lifting and little time for rest at Jon's new job make him a walking zombie for the first couple of months that he works there. He walks home from the bus stop and showers before crashing, too tired for dinner most nights. One night, Jon is so exhausted that he falls asleep on the bus and has to take another bus back to our house. I enjoy the feeling of coming home to an empty house, and Jon is so tired when he is home he sleeps most of the time he's there. With the exception of some money for the bus and lunches, Jon gives his entire first paycheck to me. With the next he pays to have a friend fix the dent on my car.

I watch as his attitude and body change with his new job. He smiles more, loses weight, and builds muscle. Seeing him look as he had in the past is harder for me than I expect it to be. It hurts to see him that way and know I don't love him anymore. I'm not sure how Jon feels and wonder if he will leave now that he has a job and a means to support himself. I almost expect it and then don't understand why he hasn't. During the year of his unemployment, Jon seemed to outright dislike me. Now he just seems pensive, never making a move to talk to me or is so neutral when he does that it is impossible for me to gauge what he might be thinking.

This new routine goes on for months. Jon becomes accustomed to the demands of his new job and is able to remain conscious past dinner time. He does not make as much as I do, but he is able to pay half of our rent which makes me feel like I can save again. We never had joint accounts. That's one thing my mother had been adamant about when we moved in together. She thought that was something we should wait to do until after we were married. While Jon was unemployed, it had not mattered much to me, but now that I am saving, I'm happy that Jon is not privy to the amount I'm able to put away.

We share cooking duties, flipping every other night and whoever doesn't cook, cleans. I may use more pans than I need from time to time. I'm still angry. Even after all of this time and even though things are so much better, Jon has never really apologized to me. I hold on to the pain and the shame he made me feel almost as a method of protecting myself from caring for him again. I don't think I will ever be able to put into words exactly how permanently he has hurt me. When he speaks to me, if he speaks to me, all I can hear is the roar of him not saying he is sorry.

To me, it's a sign of weakness that he cannot admit what he did was wrong. As though not drawing any attention to it will make it like it had never happened. That he thinks I will somehow forget. That's where he is wrong. I will never forget.

I am in the kitchen making dinner when Jon walks in one day from work. Jon checks our mail on the way home each day since he passes the bank of mailboxes on the other side of our building on his way back from the bus stop. I tense as he approaches me but then realize he is just handing me an envelope. Taking it from him, I see it is from the funeral home I had used for my parents. I am accustomed to receiving something from them, maybe quarterly, normally advertising specials on burial plots. Never too early to plan for the inevitable, I suppose. This envelope is different from all of the others, though. It is shaped liked a Hallmark card instead of the longer, thinner envelopes I received in the past.

Absentmindedly, I open the envelope and see that inside is another envelope addressed to me on behalf of the funeral home from a Kate Smith in Tampa, Florida. Smith was my mother's maiden name, but it is also such a common name it could be nothing. Curious, I turn the flame of the stovetop to simmer and sit at our small table before opening the card. Jon watches me, his brows furrowed. I shrug as I open the card, gasping as I read its contents. Jon sits next to me as I pause to look up at him with wide eyes before continuing to read.

"What is it?" he asks.

"Wait, let me finish."

I finish reading the card and immediately read it again. I drum my fingers across my lower lip as my eyes skim the page. Finally, I delicately set the card down next to me, looking up at Jon as I still drum my fingers across my lower lip. Incapable of speech, I push the card in his direction. I watch Jon's reaction to the card, seeing him look up to meet my eyes at the same place I had done the same.

"Are you going to call her?"

"I guess. I'm still just trying to wrap my brain around it."

"I'll finish dinner. Just take your time."

"You don't have to." I move to stand but Jon shakes his head and goes to the kitchen.

I toy with the corner of the card, worrying it until the different layers of paper are exposed. The card is from my grandmother, my mother's mother. The grandmother I have spent my entire life thinking is dead. Her letter. Kate

Smith. I practice saying that name in my mind. The letter from Kate Smith says that she had only learned of my parents' deaths last year. She had attempted to locate me afterward without success when she had found their obituaries and from that was able to find the address of the funeral home. She sent the card with the hope that the funeral home would still have my contact information and would forward the card to me.

A grandmother. All this time I thought I was alone in the world. Why would my mom keep this from me? The letter includes Kate Smith's telephone number. I cannot imagine calling her. What would I say? It's all too much to process. Thinking of it just makes me think of my mother and how desperately I wish she was still here. My mind is a jumble of conflicting emotions and questions all coming back to: why hadn't my mother ever told me that my grandmother was still alive? Were there other secrets she had kept from me?

Growing up, I always envied my classmates with grandparents. My dad's parents had died before I was born, and from what my mother told me, I was a toddler when her parents had passed away. I never questioned it. Why should I? It is so surreal to be accepting the fact that all that time it had been a lie. I could have had a relationship with my grandmother. Why had my mother kept that from me? What had happened to make her lie to me?

Jon brings a plate of food over to me. I look up surprised, blushing when I admit I'm not hungry anymore. Jon doesn't seem upset. He just puts it in the microwave for me in case I change my mind later on. I just cannot decide what to do. Call my grandmother or… I can't imagine not calling her. I just don't know if I can handle calling her today. This is just all so sudden. I rise quickly, thinking of something. Rushing past where Jon sits eating his dinner, I crouch down to look at the bottom shelf of our bookcase where we had stored my parents' old photo albums. Not sure which one I am thinking of, I pull three out and bring them back over to the table.

Combing through them, I find what I'm looking for: a faded Polaroid of my mother standing stiffly next my grandmother, on the front porch of a house I don't recognize. It's the only picture of Kate Smith I've ever seen. My mother looks to be about fifteen years old. I try to remember where my mother had grown up, somewhere on the East coast, maybe Pennsylvania. I look closely at the woman who is my grandmother. In the picture, she has Mary Tyler Moore hair and is wearing a simple dress with a large floral pattern on it. Her arms rest on the shoulders of my mother, and they both seem uncomfortable, my mother wearing her fake smile.

Jon walks over to look at the picture. "Are you going to call her?"

"I guess. I just don't know what to say. Do I tell her I thought she was dead?"

"She might already assume that. It's not like you tried to find her for the funeral."

Jon makes a good point. For the first time since my mother's death, I feel almost angry at her. I always thought we were so close. Why had she kept this from me?

"I'm calling her." I get up to get my phone out of my purse.

"Do you want me to stay in here?"

"Sure," I reply as I type the number into my phone and hit the call button.

I chew on the edge of my left index finger. There is a small tear in my nail that I meant to file down. My heart pounds with the first two rings. By the third ring, when there is still no answer, I calm down. Then someone answers.

"Hello?"

I take a deep breath "Hello. Is Kate Smith there?"

"Speaking. Who is this?"

"Grace Abbott."

"Who?"

"Um, Grace Abbott," I say louder and grimace at Jon.

"Grace?"

"Yes, I am Grace." I say.

"I want you to come to Florida."

"Excuse me?" I look up at Jon, shocked.

"I'm an old lady, and I want to meet you. I'll pay for the ticket."

"I have a job," I argue.

"Do they give vacations?" she questions.

"Yes, of course." I sink into my chair.

"It's settled then. When can you come?"

This is probably the oddest conversation I have ever had. Did she just say it was settled? Of course I want to meet her. I do. I just don't know if now is the right time, but she says she is old. Could this be my only opportunity?

"I don't know. I'd have to talk to my boss."

"Let me know when you do."

"Okay."

"Okay. Bye now."

"Um, bye?" I look down at my phone to see my grandmother has hung up.

I look over at Jon. "I just talked to my grandmother."

"And?"

"She wants to fly me to Florida to meet her."

His eyes widen. "Really? Are you going to go?"

I shrug. "I guess so. Maybe I should research her first to make sure she isn't a psychopath."

"How long would you go for?"

"I have to talk to my office manager. I'm not even sure how much free time I have available."

A week later, I'm on a plane to Tampa, Florida. I managed to get a week off and am more nervous than I have ever been about anything my whole life. I am not much of a traveler. From dealing with security to my cramped flight and then a layover in Atlanta, I am exhausted by the time I land in Tampa. My grandmother is sending a friend to pick me up as she no longer drives. I make my way to baggage claim and feel a bit odd introducing myself to the guy holding a sign with my name on it. He's cute, unnervingly cute. He can't be much older than me. This is my grandmother's friend?

"Ah, hi," I say giving him a little wave. "I'm Grace."

"Hi" he reaches out his hand. "I'm Ryan."

Holy crap! Is that an accent?

"Err, welcome to Tampa."

"Thanks" I blush, trying to place his accent.

"Alright. Let's see if we can locate your luggage," he says, directing me to the carousel for my flight.

Once I point out my bag, Ryan quickly retrieves it and pulls it for me, leading me out towards the parking lot. Stepping outside of the sliding doors, I have to pause for a moment to take in the temperature change. It had been sleeting when I left Cleveland. Here it was gorgeous and sunny. Ryan is a couple steps ahead of me, and seeing I am not behind him, turns to look back at me.

His face mirrors my wide grin."Beautiful, isn't it?"

"It is." I agree.

"God awful humid in the summer. You've come for a stay at just the right time."

I nod excitedly and follow him, mentally trying to remember if I packed enough shorts. Ryan has a longer stride than I do, so I have to hurry to keep up with him as he weaves his way through the parking deck. I wonder how he knows my grandmother. He kind of looks like a surfer. Do they surf in Florida? I'm trying to figure out in my head if there are even waves on this side of the panhandle. Is there a difference since it is the Gulf of Mexico and not the Atlantic? I am so distracted that I come very close to walking right into Ryan, not noticing he has stopped. Ryan is opening the back of his Wrangler. He looks back at me, his brown hair falling into his green eyes, to reach for my carryon bag.

"Well, hullo there," Ryan grins. He clearly hadn't expected me to be as close as I am.

I flush, quickly handing him my bag before going up front and getting in.

"And we're off" Ryan jokes, starting the car.

The windows are down so I pull a clip from my purse to keep my hair out of my face. This is my first time in Florida. I spend most of our drive looking out the window. The only place I have ever seen a palm tree before this was on TV or in a book. It feels tropical. I am used to congestion, but the traffic here seems so different from back home. Every other car is a Cadillac or a Lincoln, some driven by little old ladies who can barely see over the steering wheel. As we drive, Ryan tells me how he knows my grandmother. He is her next door neighbor.

"Mind if I pop into the dairy?"

"The what?" It sounded like he said diary.

"Um, the store. I just need a loaf of bread."

"Sure. I'll just wait in the car."

Ryan pulls into a Circle K. I have never heard anyone call a gas station a dairy before. He walks out not long after with bread and a quart of milk. Then we are off again. He turns into a gated neighborhood and I admire the Spanish-style ranch houses we pass. After turning onto a cul-de-sac, Ryan parks in front of a pretty little house with a yellow mailbox. I am still not sure if I'm ready to meet the grandmother I never knew I had but figure I have made it this far. It would be silly to turn back now. I walk around to the back of Ryan's car to help him with my bags. Ryan passes me my carryon while he pulls my big bag. I follow him up the drive.

Ryan walks right in the front door, booming "Kate! Where are you? I've got Grace."

My grandmother's house smells like a can of lavender air freshener, a nice smell but not the real thing. The first room is a sitting room that looks like no one ever sits in. My parents had a room like that when I was growing up, the room I was never allowed to play in unless we had company, and then it wasn't to play in but to sit politely while the grownups talked. The sitting room leads into a pretty little kitchen with a breakfast nook that opens onto a screened-in outdoor room with a pool.

"The lanai," I hear. I recognize the voice from our phone calls.

I follow Ryan out on to the pool deck.

"How lovely," I smile, looking around.

"What was that? Come closer so I can get a look at you." My grandmother is seated at a bistro table by the pool.

I approach her, not certain if I am expected to hug her or not, this being the first time we have met. My grandmother looks me up and down. I attempt to smooth the wrinkles from my slacks before pulling the clip from my hair in an attempt to look more presentable.

"You look like your mother, only her hair was brown, not blonde. You must have gotten that from your father. Come closer so I can see your eyes better."

I shoot a panicked look at Ryan, making him laugh before lowering my face to be closer to my grandmother's.

"Your mother's eyes were brown. You must have gotten your blue ones from your father as well."

"I did." Somehow, being told my own parents' appearances is annoying me. Doesn't she realize I am fully aware that my mother had brown hair and eyes? And my father had blonde hair and green, not blue, eyes.

"Well, you're a pretty little thing. Don't you think so, Ryan? Isn't my granddaughter pretty?"

I look at my feet, turning red. How embarrassing.

"You have a lovely granddaughter, Miss Kate. I'll be off so you two can get acquainted." He turns to me, "It was great to meet you, and I hope you enjoy your visit. I'll put your cases in the guest room on my way out." I blush.

"Thank you Ryan. You are a sweetheart" Kate gushes.

"Anything for my favorite lady."

After Ryan leaves, I sit on the other side of Kate. There is a plate of sliced cheese and crackers on the table and a pitcher of lemonade. I help myself as I wonder how to ask my grandmother what had happened between my mother and her. I am conscious to not fill my plate. I don't want to seem like I'm gorging myself, but I'm not sure when or what we will be having for dinner. It is mid-afternoon, and my grandmother is old. Don't older people like to eat early and be in bed by eight?

"Is it alright if I make a phone call? I just want to let my, ah, well, Jon know that I made it here safely."

"Of course."

I stand and walk over to the other end of the pool and sit on a deck chair. Jon is still at work and doesn't answer when I call. I leave him a quick message letting him know I am fine. After I hang up I realize I did not tell him I love him. I sit for a moment, trying to recall the last time I had. It has been some time. Shaking that thought from my head, I walk back over to my grandmother.

"Everything alright, dear?"

"Yes. I just left a message."

"Well, that's nice."

We spend the remainder of the afternoon like that, in silence. It's not an uncomfortable silence. I just have so many questions and am not sure how to ask them. I know I am here to meet my grandmother, and clearly, we have accomplished that. What else does she want with me for a week? Once we finish the food on the table, she gets up and begins stacking the plates and silverware. I notice the cane beside her. When Kate goes to turn with the plates in one hand, cane in the other, I stop her.

"Here, let me carry these."

"Oh, alright. Just follow me."

Standing and using a cane, my grandmother seems shorter than she had in the photo I have of her. Is that osteoporosis? Otherwise, she is on the slim side on top, while somewhat bottom heavy. Her hair is much shorter than in the picture, a silver curled coif. The clothes she wears remind me of the scrubs I wear at work: simple blue elastic pants and a printed top. I set the small tower of plates on the kitchen counter and begin rinsing the crumbs off of them before loading them into the dishwasher. Someday, I would love to have a dishwasher of my own. Kate leans up against the counter, watching me work.

When I finish, I turn to look at her. "What would you like to do now?"

"I'd like to have a bit of a lie down if it's okay with you. You're welcome to explore the house or swim in the pool. It's heated."

"Oh, thank you. Which way is the room I'm staying in?"

"Your room is the last one down that hall," she says, pointing past the kitchen. "Now if you need anything my room is on the other side of the living room."

We go our separate ways. I slow down to look at the photos on the wall of the hallway. They're of my mother as a young girl. There are also photos of a young man. I wonder who he is. In the pictures they seem close. There is one staged professional one where he sits with my mother and grandmother in matching sweaters. Do I have an uncle I never knew of as well? This all seems so strange. I continue down the hall to my room, passing a pale blue bathroom on my right before coming to my room.

I lean on the doorway before going in. It may be the prettiest spare room I have ever seen. The walls are papered with a pale, butter shade striped print. In the center of the room is a queen-sized bed with cream comforter and an antique white metal frame. The bed has a rounded look that gives hint that it's a featherbed. There is a mass of pillows at the head: four plump standard pillows behind maybe five decorative pillows, each one different. A mismatched pair of white tables are on either side of the bed, each with matching glass lamps. In the corner is a comfy looking gray armchair with a cream crocheted blanket draped across the back. Next to the chair is an oversized ornate white dresser with a mirror top. An antique tortoise shell brush and hand mirror surrounded by various perfume bottles sit on top of the dresser. My suitcase is lying on top of a bench at the end on the bed.

Pushing myself off of the doorframe, I walk into the room and begin unpacking my things. There is a small closet off to the side with free hangers and the top two drawers of the dresser are empty. Not knowing what to pack, I had possibly over packed. I just didn't know what to expect and wanted to have multiple options. I brought two sundresses and a more formal sheath-style dress. The sundresses traveled well. The sheath dress would need to be ironed if I actually want to wear it. Next I hang the dress shirts and slacks I had packed. My other clothes could go in the dresser.

I use the top drawer for my underclothes, one bathing suit, and socks. I open the next drawer to unpack t-shirts, shorts and capris. I set my toiletry bag on the dresser and extra shoes I packed in the free space beneath it. Placing my carryon inside of my larger suitcase, I store them on the floor of the closet. Before shutting the door, I look at my clothes, hoping they aren't too out of style. It has been ages since I bought anything new. I think about going for a swim but suddenly feel beat from all of my traveling and can't help but curl up on the fluffy looking bed.

It's dark outside when I blink open my eyes. I look around, not certain where I am or where to find a light switch. My hand fumbles up and down the glass lamp closest to me until I find its switch on the cord. Once the light is on, I reach for my phone to see what time it is: nine o'clock. I wonder where my grandmother is and if she's annoyed I have slept through dinner. I go to the bathroom to freshen up before heading towards the kitchen. Nearing the kitchen, I hear voices; I flush when I recognize the one with an accent.

It sounds as though they are by the pool. I head that way and peek through the doorway.

"Ah, it's Sleeping Beauty, awakened from her slumber." Ryan catches my eye and raises his beer in my direction.

My grandmother laughs and turns towards me. "Grace, come sit. Are you hungry? Let me get you some food."

"I can get it. Please, you don't have to get up."

"Oh, don't be silly." she pats me on my arm as she moves past me. "Go sit."

I bob my head and sit in the free chair between my grandmother's seat and Ryan's. As I get closer, I realize Ryan is shirtless with a towel wrapped around his waist and still damp hair. I have to tell myself not to stare more than once. A body like that and an accent? Maybe I should visit more often.

"Um, I noticed you, ah, have an accent, um, but I couldn't place it."

"Oh, right. I'm a Kiwi."

I snort. "A what?"

Ryan laughs at my reaction, running his hand through his hair. "Not the fruit. I'm from New Zealand. It's—"

"I know where New Zealand is." I cut him off. "I've just never met anyone from there."

"Didn't mean to imply you didn't. Most people assume I'm Australian."

"Never met anyone from there either, but I did see those crocodile movies."

This makes Ryan laugh again, which makes me feel a little silly. My grandmother walks back in with my plate, and I rise to take it from her, thanking her. A filet of tilapia on rice surrounded by steamed carrots and green beans. She pours me a glass of white wine to go with it. I groan in appreciation at my first bite. This may be the best thing I have ever eaten.

"Your Gran is a wonderful cook." Ryan smiles at my reaction.

I blush. I didn't realize he heard me. Meanwhile, my grandmother is telling him to hush. I listen to them chat as I quietly eat. This is commonplace for them. Ryan comes to have dinner with Kate most nights, sometimes taking a dip in her pool. He rents the house next door, and it doesn't have a pool. In exchange for pool use and home cooked meals, Ryan keeps her company and takes care of her landscaping. I can tell my grandmother adores him. I am hungrier than I think and finish my plate in no time. I wave off help from Kate and get up to rinse my plate and put it in the dishwasher.

When I come back out, I notice she has refilled my wineglass. I am not much of a drinker and already feel a bit tipsy from the first glass. That doesn't stop me from drinking it. I am on vacation.

Peering up at Ryan, I ask. "Why did you move to the U.S?"

"Guess I've got a bit of an adventurer in me and wanted to travel. I had been bumming around from place to place with some friends and came across a business opportunity here so I stayed."

"Ohhh. Where have you been?"

"All over Asia, Hawaii, then South Africa, Brazil, California, Puerto Rico, before settling here."

"This is the first time I've been outside of Ohio," I say, looking down.

"Do you want to travel?" Kate asks me.

"I really don't know. Airplanes kind of make me nervous, but I would like to go see some places, maybe Paris or Dublin."

After another thirty minutes of talking, Ryan stands to leave, admitting he has an early day the next day.

"What do you do?" I ask.

"I run a water sports rental in St. Pete. Jet skis, kayaks, and fishing boats for charter. I'm taking a small group fishing in the gulf tomorrow."

"What fun. I love the water!"

"Would you like me to take you out while you're here?"

"I don't know. I've never actually done any of those things before."

"You'll be in good hands with me."

I inhale, my eyes widening. Ryan clears his throat and looks down.

"What a wonderful idea," Kate says clapping, looking back and forth at us. "Ryan, what day works best for you?"

"Ahh, I'd have to check the calendar. Maybe the day after tomorrow." He looks at me, giving me a half smile.

"That sounds like a date," Kate says, patting me on the arm.

"A date? I, ah, have a, well, live with Jon. You see there—"

"Shhh, sweetheart. I meant like date on the calendar," Kate says, looking somewhat mischievously at me.

All I want to do is disappear. Ryan seems to be holding back a smile and leaves through the screen door, walking barefoot to his house. Kate laughs as my eyes are glued to his back as he walks away. He looks back right before walking out of view, and I quickly look away, wondering if he saw me watching him. Kate stands up, saying she is going to turn in. I follow her back into the house. As I walk back to my room, I think of all of the questions I have for my grandmother. Maybe tomorrow, after a good night of sleep, I will have an opportunity to find out what happened between her and my mom.

———

The next morning, I awake to the smell of coffee. I push myself up onto my elbows and deeply inhale. God, that smells amazing, good enough to start drinking coffee again. I take a moment to decide what to do. On one hand, I could go get some coffee, and I do really want some but, on the other hand, this may be the most comfortable bed I have ever slept in, and it feels like a disservice to leave it. I snuggle back under the covers only to give up, not being able to ignore nature's call. I head straight to the bathroom. Checking myself out in the mirror, I pull my hair back into a messy bun at my nape. I had slept in an old pair of scrub pants and a concert tee. Off in search of coffee, I pad barefoot to the kitchen.

Kate is at the counter cutting a grapefruit in half. Raising one half, she asks if I want any.

"Sure." I peer at the coffeemaker. It looks fancy, and I can't tell if it is done yet. "Coffee ready?"

"It is," Kate says, pulling a cup down from a cabinet and handing it to me.

I pour myself a cup and hold it right under my nose to smell. Nothing like the smell of fresh coffee. Sometimes I wonder what I prefer: the smell or the taste. After adding a dollop of milk, I take a small sip, trying not to burn my tongue. Kate has a tray of muffins and fruit that I take from her, making her tsk at me. I shrug and follow her out to the pool. Setting the tray on the table, I hurry back inside to retrieve my coffee. I don't want it to feel abandoned. Kate laughs at my near embrace of my mug. I had gotten out of the habit of drinking coffee in the morning, but I'm looking forward to picking it back up. As we eat, I push my fears aside and ask Kate point blank what had happened between her and my mother.

Kate pushes her plate away and steeples her hands on

the table in front of her. I pause to watch her, noticing her hands tremble.

"That, my dear, is a long story."

"I've got a week" I try to joke.

"That you do." She brings one of her hands up to finger the wisps of fine hairs along her scalp. "I just wonder if you'll want to leave early once I tell you." her eyes seem wet and her voice hushed.

I reach out to touch her arm, suddenly feeling guilty for asking. "I'm sorry. I just can't help but wonder why I didn't know about you."

"It's alright dear. Don't apologize." Kate pushes her chair back and stands.

"You haven't finished eating. Please come sit back down."

"Oh, I'm not going far," Kate murmurs as she sits on a wicker-style loveseat a few feet from the table. "I just like to be busy when I talk." She pulls a bundle of yarn with two needles sticking out if it from a basket that sits below the loveseat.

She pulls the needles from the bundle, careful not to drop any of the stitches and begins to knit. Once she knits a couple stitches, she looks up at me, her hands still busy and says, "Your mother stopped talking to me after I tried to convince her to leave your father and give you up for adoption."

I gasp.

"I want you to know, my dear, that I have regretted that for twenty-five years."

"Why would you tell her to do that?"

"Well, I was just scared she would end up like me, and I also didn't like the idea of her leaving me behind. I had no right to put that much pressure on your mother. I'm not sure if your mother ever told you much about me or her life growing up." Kate eyes search mine.

I shake my head and look down.

Kate blinks a few times, taking a shaky breath and goes on. "I see. Well, I married very young, too young. I was a lovesick fool, and your grandfather was a good-for-nothing. We got married when I found out I was pregnant with Ronald, and not long after, your mother was born. Your grandfather left us. Here I was, all on my own, with two little ones. I moved back in with my parents, which was a nightmare because now, not only was I a disgrace, I was also divorced. In those days, that was a very bad thing."

As I listen to her speak, she never slows her pace, needles clicking. Row after row of, well I'm not quite sure what she is making, but am amazed at how fast she goes with barely a glance down.

"Living with my parents was awful. Trying to get out of their house is what had pushed me into the arms of your grandfather in the first place. My mother watched your mother and uncle while I went to work. I managed to scrape enough together to get my own place. My mother kept watching them while I worked but at least I was out of their house. I waitressed and worked like a dog. It was not a life I would wish on anyone, but somehow I made due. Once your mother and uncle were old enough to keep watch of themselves, I stopped taking them to my parents. Happy to once and for all be free of them, I also swore off men. I had plenty sniffing around, but men led to babies and I had enough of those already." Kate motions for me to pass her unfinished plate to her. Setting her knitting on her lap, she takes a bite of her muffin and puts the plate on the seat next to her.

Once she finishes chewing, she goes on. "Your uncle

Ronny was a bit of a trouble maker. He was always up to no good. Anne tried to keep up with him, but Ronny was almost two years older than her and your mother was on the small side, even as a child. I was at work when it happened." Kate pauses again, setting her knitting in her lap once more to pick up a napkin to dab the corners of her eyes. Tears keep forming so she looks up at the ceiling and blinks rapidly before going on. "Ronny had built a fort out of old boards he came across on his escapades, high up in an oak tree. It made your mother so angry that she was so small and couldn't climb up there with him. She used to sit cross-legged at the bottom of the tree and wait for him to come down. While I was at work one day, a board broke, and Ronny fell out of the tree. He landed right in front of your mother and broke his neck."

Kate sets her knitting to the side and grabs her cane to stand. Placing one shaking hand on her hip, she randomly pats it. "Your mother didn't leave him. She was too little to understand that he was dead. It was maybe hours later when I got home from work and went looking for them. When I first saw them, it just looked like Ronny was lying on his belly looking at a bug or something." Kate takes a deep breath and starts pacing slowly along the pool deck, still patting her hip with her hand, almost like setting a rhythm for her words to follow. "I didn't think anything was wrong until I saw Anne crying. I started hollering at Ronny to get up and Anne just looked up at me shaking her little face, saying 'Mama, mama, mama.' I fell to my knees and turned him over. He was lifeless in my arms, already cold, and heavy. I think people heard me screaming because the next thing I knew my father was pulling me off of him and my mother was holding Anne."

Kate takes another napkin off the tray, and after wiping her eyes, blows her nose before sitting back down. I am oblivious to my own tears as I sit next to my grandmother and put my hand on her arm. I want to hug her but feel uncertain, having only met her the day before. Kate reaches a hand up to wipe the tears from my eyes and then pats my hand.

"I never even knew I had an uncle," I say, sniffling. "How old was he?"

"Ronny was nine. Your mother was seven. I had a very hard time dealing with losing Ronny. Your mother and I moved back in with my folks because I could not manage to work after that. Your mother, if possible, took it even worse. To her, Ronny hung the moon. She used to follow him everywhere. Now that he was gone, she seemed lost. I wasn't much help. I understand that now. I was the adult and should have paid more attention to her grief. I can't claim to have been much of a mother after that. Your mother slowly came around with no help from me. If anything, she took care of me. Five years later, I managed to go back to work and was set on staying at my parent's house this time around. It was just easier that way, and your mother and mine got on so I just stayed."

Kate picks her knitting back up, and I lean my head on a pillow of my hands on the back of the loveseat. "Your mother met your father when she was sixteen years old. She hated him. I think he bullied someone, but your mother, little thing that she was, scared the crap out of him and stopped him. After that, she could not get rid of him. He was like some lovesick puppy that could not leave her be. It wore her down eventually, and before I knew it, every time I turned around I was tripping over them kissing. They didn't even try to sneak around. It was as though someone sewed their lips together. My father was old-fashioned, and it drove him nuts. I wasn't happy about it, either. Anne was only seventeen when she found out she was pregnant with you. I could see history repeating itself and your father leaving her just like your grandfather had left me. I tried to talk your mother into going to college and giving you up for adoption, but her heart was set on marrying your father. I just could not believe it would work out and told her so. We were both stubborn, and I told her I never wanted to see her again if she went through with it. That is my greatest regret."

"Your father had a friend who had moved out to Ohio and offered them a place to stay. I tried sending your mother letters over the years, but they all came back return to sender. I know now your father was a good man and didn't leave her. I only wish I would have trusted that then. I know your mother never forgave me for what I did, and now that she's gone, well, I hope maybe we can have a chance to still be family."

"I'm sorry you never had the chance to talk with her again. I'm sorry she sent your letters back."

"Shh, sweetheart," Kate says, patting me on the cheek. "In time, I will be with Anne and Ronny again."

After our talk, Kate admits to being overtired and needing to lie down. I clear the table and load the dishwasher. I think about putting my suit on and going for a swim but after sitting on my bed decide a bit of rest is in order. I replay the conversation in my head. I cannot imagine how Kate or my mom dealt with Ronny's death. Picturing my mother, only seven years old, with his body breaks my heart. I also cannot understand why my mother had kept all of this from me. I wonder if my father even knew about Ronny. Part of me can understand Kate's advice to do an adoption. My mother had been so young.

I cringe, remembering the very in-depth birds and bees talk I had been subjected to as an adolescent. Had my mother worried the same thing would happen to me? Thinking about it, she did seem to be very pushy about me getting on the pill before I even contemplated having sex for the first time. Even considering all of that, I can't understand why my mother would still refuse to reconcile with Kate. I know she was stubborn, but to keep my own grandmother from me seemed overly harsh. Is there more to the story, I wonder as I fall asleep.

When I wake up the next morning, I consider pulling back the fitted sheet to check the brand of the featherbed. I seriously need one back home. This is the most comfortable bed I have ever slept on. My stomach rumbles as I stretch, reminding me that I missed lunch and dinner the day before. Walking to the kitchen, I feel bad for sleeping through two meals in as many days. I pause at the photo hanging in the hallway. I lean in to look at Ronny. This picture must have been taken not long before his death. My heart breaks a little looking at his impish grin.

My grandmother is sitting on the wicker loveseat, knitting.

"What are you making?"

"It's a prayer shawl. I'm part of a knitting group at my church. We knit these shawls and then the pastor prays over them, and we give them to people going through a rough time."

"It's very pretty."

"Thank you. Do you knit?"

I shake my head, reaching out to touch the shawl.

"My group meets tomorrow and since you'll be spending the day with Ryan I'm going to go. So I'm trying to finish it.

"Oh, right…"

"He's a very handsome young man isn't he?"

I look at her, confused.

"Ryan" she answers the question I didn't ask.

"Kate…"

"Okay, I'll stop. Hungry?"

My stomach answers for me. I don't let Kate get up to make me something, telling her to keep knitting and just let me know what I can have. She grumbles about me not being very easy to wait on and tells me there is lunch meat and cheese in the fridge. I make myself a sandwich with some chips on the side and grab a soda before heading back outside. I still cannot get over how pleasant it is compared to Ohio this time of year. We chat while I eat, keeping to easy topics, neither of us prepared to revisit the emotional discussion of yesterday morning.

Sometime after lunch, I change into my swimsuit and try out the pool. It is a bit strange to be swimming outside this time of year, but the water feels wonderful. I'm dozing in an armchair-style float when a splash wakes me. Blinking, I look around trying to place the source of the splash, locking eyes with Kate who is still sitting on the loveseat. How strange, I think to myself. Suddenly, I'm in midair as someone flips my float. I come up sputtering and wiping water from my eyes to see Ryan standing in front of me laughing. Ryan is clearly not expecting me to pounce on him. I dunk him in the water, causing him to do some sputtering of his own.

My eyes widen at his mischievous expression as he charges me. I squeal, "No, no, no!" But it's useless as his hands circle my waist and he pulls me under. As we're coming back up, I kick his legs out from under him before fleeing to the other end of the pool. With my back up against the wall and just my head above the water, I keep my eyes on Ryan. He puts his hands up in defeat and slowly swims over to me.

He's laughing. "Sorry about flipping you. I couldn't resist."

"None of that tomorrow."

Ryan leans in and whispers, "No promises," in my ear.

I pray he doesn't see me shiver and try to seem riveted by the cuticle of my thumb to avoid looking at him.

"So where are you taking Grace tomorrow?" Kate asks.

"That, Kate, is a surprise."

I can't help but flush and look up at him then. He grins at me, lifting his brows up and down a couple of times, making her laugh.

"Just bring her back in one piece," Kate says, getting up to start dinner.

"Oh, let me help," I say, swimming over to the ladder and climbing out. I can feel Ryan's eyes on my back. I grab my towel and walk inside, doing my best not to drip everywhere. Kate is making a chicken casserole and lets me make the side salad. Once the chicken is in the oven and the salad in the fridge, we go back outside. Ryan is just climbing out of the pool. I stop mid-step to watch the water bead and roll down his chest. Kate, who is standing behind me, clears her throat to bring me back down to earth. I feel flustered at the thought of spending the day with him tomorrow, wondering if I will make an ass out of myself.

Ryan drinks a beer while Kate and I share a bottle of wine with dinner. The chicken is just as good as the tilapia from the first night. I'm going to have to try and learn what I can from Kate in the kitchen over the next few days. Over dinner, Ryan tells us all about the group he had taken fishing that day. With tourists, he mainly does catch and release. Only the truly serious sport fishermen want to preserve some of their catches. He even has a buddy he could refer them to should they want them mounted for display. I am curious about what he has planned for the next day. Ryan tells me to be ready by nine and to wear my suit. Flashbacks of his hands on my waist make me gulp, causing Kate to glance at me.

Ryan leaves not long after dinner. I clean up after Kate goes to bed and then head to bed myself. I lie there, thinking of my mother and what it must have been like having Kate as a mom and no dad. I wonder what happened to Kate after my mother left. They had lived in Pennsylvania at the time. How had Kate ended up in Florida?

I wake with a start the next morning, grabbing my phone to see how much time I have to get ready before Ryan arrives. I have two hours. Not thinking Kate is up yet, I take a shower and get dressed. Pulling on my same suit from the day before, I struggle over what to wear over it, settling on some running shorts that dry easily and a white V-neck t-shirt, hopeful the white will reflect the sun. I had packed plenty of sunscreen and wonder if it is too early to apply, deciding to hold off I set the bottle next to my purse before walking out to the kitchen. Kate is up and has just started a pot of coffee when I walk in.

I freeze when I see what she is putting into the oven. Cinnamon rolls, my mother's recipe. I guess the recipe is actually Kate's. I can't help but feel pulled back to the last time I made them. How excited I had been to do something sweet for Jon and how he had thrown them against the wall. Kate is looking at me. I force a smile and make myself a cup of coffee. We eat by the pool and then Kate leaves to get ready for her knitting club. One of the members will be picking her up around eleven. I am happy that my visit will not make her miss her meeting. She seems to really enjoy her knitting. She had finished the shawl the night before, after dinner. I picked it up from the arm of the loveseat and unfold it. It's a plum shade of purple and has a diamond-like pattern to it with ribbed edging. I gather it in my arms, saying my own little prayer for whoever will receive it before refolding it and setting it back down.

Ryan comes over not long after Kate's finished getting ready, opening the front door and shouting, "Hullo," before walking in.

"We're out back," Kate calls out.

Ryan is wearing loose green swim shorts that hang low on his hips and a bluc t-shirt. I try hard not to look at his waist.

He checks out what I'm wearing. "Wearing togs under that?"

"Huh?"

"Oh right. Sorry," he says, lifting his arm up to scratch the back of his neck, exposing a bit of his abs. "Your suit."

"Um." I'm trying not to drool. "Yes, I am wearing my suit," I say, lifting my shirt, wondering why his eyes just dilated.

"Ready?"

"Should I put on sunscreen? I have some on my face, but since it isn't summer, I wasn't sure about the rest of me."

"Sure, wouldn't want you to burn."

I go to my room to get the sunscreen and take off my shirt. Once back in the kitchen I ask Ryan if he will help me get my back. He gives me a cheeky grin, motioning with his finger for me to turn around. Ryan starts with my shoulders, almost massaging them as he moves to the back of my neck. I have to control myself from dipping my head back onto him as his long fingers work the lotion in. Ryan squeezes more lotion into his hands before rubbing my arms. My eyes are closed as his hands are on me, but when I open them he is standing right in front of me, holding out the bottle.

I blush when he says, "You should probably do your front and legs."

Yes, that is a good idea, I think, taking the bottle from him to finish up before putting my shirt back on. Per his recommendation, I am wearing simple sneakers.

"Should I bring anything?"

"Nope. I've got it covered."

Kate tells us to have fun, winking at me, and asks if we will be home by dinner. Ryan says he wouldn't dream of eating anywhere else, which makes Kate happy. As we walk up to his Wrangler, I grin when I see two kayaks on his roof. I have always wanted to try this.

"So where are you taking me?"

"Someplace wet," Ryan laughs.

"Silly Kiwi."

"Hey, well done!"

"I thought you were crazy when you said it," I admit.

We've been in the car sometime before I groan "I forgot my sunglasses."

"Not a problem" Ryan says, reaching to the floor board behind me, producing a worn looking baseball cap and hands it to me.

I flip the visor mirror open and put it on, pulling my pony tail through the opening in the back. The hat is huge on me.

"Is it okay if I adjust it?" Jon had gotten angry at me once when I had done that to one of his hats without asking first.

Ryan gives me a strange look and nods.

The hat has a strap you can use to tighten it with on the back. I make it as small as I can. It is still a bit big on me but will work. Once I have my hair pulled through, I turn to Ryan and smile. He laughs, pushing the bill down so I can't see him anymore.

"Hey!" As much as I protest, I have to admit I am drawn to Ryan. Why does that make me feel so guilty?

Bargaining

a transaction, situation, or event regarded in the light of its results
-Merriam Webster

We head west towards St. Petersburg, crossing the Howard Frankland Bridge. Ryan takes me to the dock at his business. It's called Erickson Gulf Water Sports. We stop by the front office first so he can introduce me to the kids who get folks checked in and manage any release forms and payments. They all seem so young, maybe just out of high school. I'm surprised when a couple of employees seem to recognize my name. Did he talk about me to them? I stand there, politely making small talk, while he carries the kayaks down to the dock. I wave goodbye to everyone when he calls me over.

I hold my breath as he buckles me into a lifejacket. I probably could have done that myself but make no move to stop him. As he is adjusting the strap tighter on one side, our eyes connect and I giggle, making him smile. When he's finished, he tugs on my vest, making me fall into him. When I gasp, he claims he's just checking to make sure it's tight enough. He turns his head too quickly for me to tell if he is smiling or not. He holds my kayak flush to the dock as I step into it. I feel so awkward trying to keep my balance, terrified I will tip over. Thankfully, I don't, and when he passes me the paddle. I'm able to paddle out a couple of feet to give him room to get into his kayak. I can't help but watch as he does it so easily, much more gracefully than I had. Then, we are off. Ryan is an adorable tour guide, pointing out things along the way.

I have never kayaked before but get the hang of it quickly. One thing I did not expect is how much water drips onto me with each pull of my paddle. Ryan doesn't get as wet. I try holding the paddle farther from my body, but that doesn't seem to work. I give up and am just happy that I'm wearing a swimsuit. I wonder if Ryan thinks I'm doing a good job. I think I'm keeping up with him just fine, or is he taking it easy on me?

Ryan suddenly gets very animated and points over to our right. I squint, not seeing anything. I shrug and shake my head but Ryan's insistent finger continues to point at the water. I look again, just in time to see a large, white something break the surface.

"What is that?" I shriek.

"Don't be frightened, love. It's just a manatee," Ryan says, laughing at my reaction.

All I can think of as I watch the manatee slowly sink back under the water is that Ryan just called me love, and how sexy it sounded. Everything he says sounds sexy. My attraction towards Ryan is making me feel flustered, not that it matters. He lives in Florida, and I live in Ohio. With Jon. I wonder what I will feel when I see Jon again when he comes to pick me up from the airport. It's wild to think my trip is already half over. I have learned so much but still have so many questions for my grandmother. What I cannot understand most of all is why my mother had never forgiven her.

Ryan is giving me a weird look. Oh Lord. Has he been talking to me this whole time? I must have seemed like a complete space cadet.

"Sorry. I wasn't listening. Can you repeat that?" I ask.

He shrugs it off and doesn't say anything. I sigh, worried I have hurt his feelings. Not knowing what else to do and wanting to lighten the mood, I angle my paddle in his direction and splash him. His mouth drops open, forming an O as in, "Oh no, you didn't." I squeal as he quickly maneuvers over to me.

"Don't flip me! Please don't flip me!" I plead.

Ryan has his kayak right on the side of mine, facing the opposite direction with one hand gripping the side. I put my hand on top of his trying to pry off his fingers. Ryan keeps looking down at his hand and then to my face before holding both hands up in surrender. Then, back paddling away from me, he leans towards me and in a hushed tone, with a twinkle in his eyes, promises there will be payback. I roll my eyes, trying to act like I'm not scared as he just shakes his head at me.

We paddle a bit further. By this time, my shoulders are feeling a bit sore. Ryan notices me rolling them and asks if I want to head back. I ask if we can just drift a bit before going back, and Ryan likes that idea. Being on the water is incredibly peaceful. Ryan explains that because of the manatees only boats without motors are allowed. The manatees tend to stay close to the surface and in the past some had been injured. Since they are a protected species, this is one way of keeping them safe. I cannot imagine trying to kayak in the same place boats or jet skis are going. I'm still nervous about tipping and am grateful the water is so much calmer here.

I set my paddle down in front of me, and Ryan points out a zip tie on the side I can wrap around it to make sure it won't fall in the water. It won't be a huge deal if I do drop the paddle, though, because it has a float attached. With the paddle secure, I take off Ryan's hat and lean back in my seat, closing my eyes and enjoying the sun on my face. I can feel the water gently lapping on the sides of my kayak as it rocks me, like a cradle. If I'm not careful I could easily fall asleep. This is the coolest thing I have done in a long time. I fill my lungs with fresh air and stretch my arms out in front and then behind me. I'll be lucky if I can lift anything tomorrow.

After some time, I raise my head back up and open my eyes, blinking at the brightness before putting Ryan's hat back on and looking around for him. He's somewhat behind me now, just watching me. I blush, wondering if I dozed off there for a second.

"Are you hungry?"

"Starved," I confess.

"Burgers sound good?"

"They sound great!"

I follow him back towards the dock. My arms ache, but I feel invigorated, and I can't stop smiling. Back at the dock Ryan gets out first, tugging his kayak out of the water before coming to help steady mine so I can get out. The dock is wet so when I step on it my foot slides out from under me, and I land on my other knee, hard. I crawl the rest of the way onto the dock. Ryan quickly tugs my kayak onto the dock before rushing to check on me. My knee has a nasty scrape and is bleeding, my hand holding it tightly. Tears are forming in my eyes, but I do my best to blink them away.

Ryan crouches down next to me, and I move my hand a little so he can see the wound before covering it again.

Without a word, Ryan scoops me up in one easy movement and carries me to the office. I feel a little silly, thinking I probably could have walked, but when I try to tell Ryan, I can't seem to spit it out. When we get to the office, Ryan sets me on the counter, waving off his employees while he retrieves a first aid kit. While my scrape is mainly superficial, there seems to be a lot of blood. Ryan gently coaxes me into taking my hand off my knee.

I study him as he gently washes my knee then applies ointment. It takes two large bandages to cover it, and as Ryan smoothes the second one on me, his fingertips on my skin make me erupt in goose bumps. I shiver, suddenly cold. With his hands on my waist, Ryan helps me off the counter. I walk gingerly to the bathroom to wash the blood off my hands and use a paper towel to wipe my shin. Ryan is putting away the first aid supplies when I walk back out. I can't help but notice the trail of blood drips across his floor. I'm mortified. "Ryan, I am so sorry. Here, let me clean up." I reach for a roll of paper towels.

"Don't be silly. Sit." He wheels a chair over to me. "This will just take a moment." Once he finishes, he comes back to check on me. "Are you sure you're alright?"

I nod, feeling like such an idiot having just watched him clean the floor.

"Still up for a burger?" Ryan asks.

I pout, nodding again.

"Has your injury caused you to become mute?"

I tap my index finger on my lips, trying to look like I'm thinking about it but am unable to keep a straight face. Ryan reaches out his hand to help me up. I shake my head. I will probably have a bruise, but I'm not an invalid. He checks a few things in the office before we leave. Once in his Jeep, we pass at least six burger places before Ryan stops at a kind of rundown looking place. I shoot him a concerned look.

"Don't judge. Best burger ever. Besides I drove so you're stuck either way," Ryan says, walking around to open my door.

"Oh, I see how it is."

"They have milkshakes."

"Sign me up."

"Atta girl."

The place is seat yourself. Ryan leads us over to a booth. When I ask for a menu, Ryan laughs and points to the wall behind me. Turning, I see the back wall is one giant chalkboard-style menu.

"How cool," I say, getting up to take a closer look.

Ryan, clearly already certain of what he's ordering, stays put. The burgers are ordered by size with a million different topping options. My eyes light up when I see artichoke as one of them. I've never had them on a burger before, and it sounds so good. I walk back to our booth, ready to order. Not long after, a waitress comes over. Ryan orders a half-pound, medium cooked burger with lettuce, tomatoes, cheese and banana peppers, plus a chocolate milkshake. I order a quarter-pound, medium cooked burger with the same toppings as Ryan, just artichokes instead of banana peppers and a mint chocolate chip milkshake. Ryan crinkles his nose at my topping selection and orders a basket of onion rings for us to split.

Our milkshakes come out first, topped with whipped cream and a cherry. I have to pace myself or I'll be done with my milkshake before the food comes out. While we wait, Ryan asks me about twenty times how my knee is. The last time he gets the hint when I kick him in the shin under the table doing my best to look innocent while sipping on my shake. Ryan changes the subject and starts asking me about Ohio. I consider not telling him about Jon but feel as though the omission could be considered a lie. I try not to notice how Ryan seems to stiffen when I say I live with my boyfriend. Not wanting to talk about him further, I tell Ryan about my job and the Cuyahoga River, wondering out loud if people kayak on it.

"So you'd like to go out on a yak again?"

"A yak?"

"Term of affection."

"Oh, I see. Yes, I would, even though I'm not sure I'll be able to lift my arms tomorrow, and I will have to work on my dismount."

"How does your knee feel?"

"It's fine. I feel a bit silly you had to carry me and even with my fall I had a great time. The water was beautiful. Really, thank you so much for taking me."

Conversation ceases for a bit once our food arrives. Hands down the best burger I have ever had. It's so thick I follow Ryan's lead and squish it before trying to take a bite. The onion rings are amazing as well. The perfect level of crispiness. I'm happy this place isn't a chain or I'd fear for my arteries. I ask Ryan what made him settle down in Florida. It seems somewhat tame after all the places he talked about. It turns out the owner of the house he rents is an old friend he'd done some of his traveling with. They had come up with the idea of the business together, and since his friend is wealthy, he said he would put up the investment if Ryan ran the place. His friend is American and wanted to keep the business stateside.

"So where's your friend?"

"Jack pops in from time to time, but he never stays long. Bit of a gypsy. I think he's in Indonesia right now."

"Do you wish you were with him?"

"I love to travel, and there are still many places I want

to see. I usually try and take one trip a year, but I like sleeping in my own bed."

"Someday I'd like to travel, maybe go outside of the US."

"What's stopping you?"

"Work, money, fear of the unknown."

"And your Jon? Does he like to travel?"

I shrug, uncomfortable that I don't even know the answer to that. While Ryan may think it's a strange, non-answer, he doesn't push. After finishing our food and paying the check, we stand to leave. When Ryan notices me grimace he talks me into letting him double check my bandages once we are at the car. I patiently sit in the passenger seat, my legs facing out as Ryan inspects my knee. I try explaining to him that I'm fine and that it's just stiff and all I need to do is put ice on it once we get back to Kate's, but Ryan isn't convinced. I don't press it; I'm enjoying his hands on my legs too much, wondering if maybe he's making a big deal just so he can touch me. I shake off the idea of him being interested in me; he's just a nice guy. Since my bleeding had stopped ages ago, Ryan finally admits an ice pack is a good idea and looks guilty when he warns me I'll probably have a nasty bruise.

"Ryan, seriously. Relax. I bruise easy. It's not a big deal. I'm a total klutz."

"So Grace is not very graceful?"

"No," I laugh. "I most certainly am not."

Ryan thinks this is funny and teases me about it most of the way home, asking me for examples of my klutziest moments. I have plenty to share. My story about crashing a Segway on a rogue speed bump almost makes him cry, he is laughing so hard. I can't help but laugh, his laughter is contagious. I stress how much it hurt at the time but that only makes him crack up more, until I find myself shaking with laughter along with him. After I catch my breath I tell him how I had been with my parents and can still remember how angry my father had gotten at the rental guy. At the time, I didn't have health insurance and had been happy and felt lucky I had not broken anything. I had jumped up after my crash, checking myself for broken bones and said I'm fine, I'm good over and over. Looking back, I'm not sure if I was trying to convince my father or myself.

When we get back to my grandmother's house, I take a quick shower and change into some khaki shorts and a tank. Then Ryan gets me all set on a lounge chair with an ice pack. I'm unsuccessful trying to take care of myself, and once Ryan tells Kate about my knee, she gangs up on me as well. As much as I fight the attention, I secretly enjoy it, knowing Jon would not have spared my knee a second glance. Once they're satisfied I am comfortable, Kate gets us all caught up on gossip from her knitting group, excited to announce the grandson of one of the members is getting married.

She turns to me. "When will we hear wedding bells for you, Grace?"

I flush, shaking my head. Ryan cocks his head to the side, looking at me.

Kate continues. "Well, why not?"

"I'd really rather not talk about it." I fiddle with the hem of my tank top, not able to look at either of them.

"Aw, leave her be, Kate." Ryan seems to sense my discomfort.

I can tell Kate wants to say something else and am grateful Ryan interceded on my behalf. Kate grumbles and gets up to check the roast she is making for dinner. Once she is out of sight, I mouth "thank you" to Ryan. He dips his head in acknowledgement, but I can see a question remains in his eyes. I don't want either of them to know how unhappy I am. I don't want to give Kate a reason to worry now that she's found me and the idea of admitting to Ryan that I'm in a loveless relationship is embarrassing. I clear my throat and look away when I see his eyes are still on me.

Given my invalid status, Ryan helps Kate set the table and bring out the food. At first, they think I should eat where I am sitting so I can keep my leg elevated and the ice on it. I put my foot down, literally, and argue that I can ice my knee again later and had been just fine sitting in a booth at lunch. I win the right to sit like a normal person at the table. Ryan opens a bottle of red wine. It surprises me when he pours himself a glass, having only seen him drink beer with dinner. Ryan confesses he does not like white wine.

Kate again has outdone herself with the meal. Over my first and second serving, I ask her how she ended up in Florida. She explains that when my mother became pregnant with me my parents moved from Pennsylvania to Ohio. Kate lived with her parents, now taking care of them in their old age. Her father had been a successful businessman and as long as she stayed in their home she had no need to work. My great grandfather died when I was around two years old; my great grandmother three years later. As the sole beneficiary of their estate and still estranged from my mother, Kate had wanted nothing more than to get out of Pennsylvania.

Tired of the cold weather and wanting to live near water, she decided on Florida. She had friends who wintered there. She had no interest in being a snow bird and having two homes to maintain, so she took the plunge and moved down full time. She questioned her sanity at first in making such a move. She paused before asking me if I had ever heard of a palmetto bug. I shake my head, looking over at Ryan as he starts laughing. Kate explains they are large, flying cockroach-looking bugs that seemed to be everywhere. I don't want to believe her at first, but Ryan, while laughing, assures me they are very real.

Kate made a go of it, though, and built a life for herself in Florida. She didn't have to work but took a job as a secretary at a church. Now, she has a good group of friends, counting Ryan among them. She is also friends with Jack, since they've been neighbors for ten years. Before Ryan lived there Kate was often in charge of collecting Jack's mail for him while he globe trotted. When Ryan moved into his house, Jack made it part of the rental agreement that he maintain the landscaping of Kate's property as well. Ryan liked yard work, and it gave him an opportunity to befriend Kate. She always had a glass of lemonade ready for him, and he could use her pool.

Once Kate got to know him better, the lemonade got ditched for Belgian beer, and he started joining her for dinner. Kate liked the company and having someone to cook for, and Ryan had never eaten as well in his life. When I ask about his mother's cooking, he admits it's vile shit, apologizing to Kate quickly for cursing and assuring us he eats it anyway out of respect for his mum. Kate just looks pleased he enjoys her cooking so much. Looking at them, I envy their easy relationship and how comfortable Ryan is with my grandmother. It's amazing to me how attached I feel to them, considering I've only known them for such a short time.

I am already feeling sad that my trip is almost half over. When I leave, Ryan will continue his evening dinners and friendship with my grandmother and where will I be? In Ohio, carefully walking up slippery steps to avoid breaking my neck, sleeping in the same bed with someone

I used to love. I ponder if the spark of attraction I feel for Ryan might in some way have turned my senses back on to that feeling. That maybe when I get home to Jon, things will be like they had in the beginning when we could barely keep our hands off each other. Everywhere we went, Jon found a patch of exposed skin to caress, the back of my neck, the top of my knee, the inside of my wrist. I had been just as bad, especially with kisses, never being able to stop with just one.

There is something about being at my grandmother's house that makes me want to stomp my feet and throw a childlike tantrum and yell at the top of my lungs, "I don't want to go home! I want my grandmother." I keep those urges within, but after a piece of chocolate cake, I sit next to Kate as she knits on her little wicker loveseat and lean into her. Since Ryan also drank wine with us that evening, the bottle had not lasted long. He opens another bottle and fills both of our glasses. I have never been much of a drinker and have drank almost nothing in the past year. This being my third glass of the evening, I'm feeling the effects.

My eyes feel heavy, and I giggle frequently. Ryan studies me as I try to regain composure then asks me out of the blue why marriage isn't for me. I blurt out, "I don't love him." Realizing what I said I clap my hand over my mouth, eyes wide. I giggle as if it's the funniest thing I have ever said, not noticing when my laughs turn into tears. Kate stashes her knitting and pulls me into a hug. Ryan goes inside to fetch some tissues. I shyly take the box from him, wishing to dissolve into the cushion instead of answering the question in his eyes.

Kate, never one to hold back, delicately, asks. "Why are you still with him?"

"I forgot how to be without him."

"Grace, that's no reason to stay with someone."

I'm now hiccupping as I speak. "I couldn't leave him when he didn't have a job."

"So you were supporting him?"

I nod, dabbing my nose.

"Is he working now?"

"Mm hmm."

"Are you happy?"

My face crumples, and I am too embarrassed to respond so I get up to go to my room. Before I can make it into the house, Ryan is there, pulling me into a hug. I bury my face into his chest as he wraps his arms around me, his mouth by my ear gently murmuring, "Shhh, shhh." After a moment, self awareness hits me. I feel foolish and stiffen in his arms. Sensing my discomfort, Ryan opens his arms and places his hands on my arms, rubbing up and down as if trying to warm me.

I pull both my top and lower lip into my mouth and bite them, closing my eyes, head tilted to the ceiling. I release my lips. "I'm just going to head to bed."

"Are you sure, dear?" Kate looks at me and then Ryan, then back at me.

Ryan pulls his hands back, putting them in his back pockets, taking a step back to unblock the doorway to the kitchen. I nod and flee. Once in my room, I pull on my pajamas and lie across my bed to finish crying without an audience. Maybe twenty minutes later, there is a soft knock at my door.

I wipe my eyes before saying, "Come in."

Ryan peeks his head in the doorway. "I brought ice."

I scoot back against my pillows, straightening out my leg as Ryan sits on the edge of my bed.

"We might want to take the bandages off and let it breathe."

I nod, reaching to do it myself, but Ryan brushes my hands away so I smirk at him and fold them on my lap. He slowly rolls the leg of my scrubs up to uncover my knee. He's careful as he eases the bandages off. It doesn't hurt at all until the final bit of adhesive pulls some skin from the sensitive area under my knee, making me flinch. Ryan's hands freeze, his eyes flicking up to the pained expression on my face. It only hurts for a moment, and since the bandage is now off, Ryan looks back down to inspect my knee. He puts his hands under my leg to lift it a bit. His hands are still cold from the ice, and I shiver. He pulls the throw blanket off the corner chair to wrap around me.

"Better?"

I know his question isn't just about being cold. I nod.

He smiles and wraps the ice around my knee. "You should probably keep that on your knee for at least fifteen minutes. Want me to keep you company?"

"Oh, you don't have to."

"It's alright. I don't mind."

"Okay." I twist my fingers absentmindedly under the blanket, feeling very nervous with Ryan still sitting on my bed. I'm not a pretty crier and can only imagine how splotchy my face must look.

We sit there for a few moments, both of us on my bed. I'm not sure what to say, and he isn't saying anything. The silence that hangs between us begins to feel almost solid. I start to ask him something. He speaks up at the same time, so we both stop, laughing, telling the other person to go ahead. Ryan insists I go first.

"Do you have brothers or sisters back in New Zealand?"

"I have two older sisters. One is still in New Zealand. The other now lives in Australia."

"Do you miss them?"

"They were a bit older than me so they acted more like second mothers than sisters. I was a bit spoiled." He smiles as though he remembers something and goes on. "They both have husbands and kids of their own now. Jean, my oldest sister, came out here with her family last year for a visit. Orlando isn't far, and they went to meet Mickey Mouse."

"Nieces and nephews?"

"Yep. Jean has two boys. Um, one is sixteen and the other maybe twelve. Nancy has a girl and a boy. Stacy is fourteen and Adam nine. I think that's about right, give or take a year."

"Are you close to them?"

"Jean's oldest had his heart set on moving out here to work with me over the summer. I wasn't up to it."

"Why not?"

"Ugh. That kid thinks he's a lady's man of some sort right now. No, thank you. I'm waiting for his hormones to settle down before I even think about it."

"No way! He can't be that bad."

"My sister is convinced he's going to knock up half his class."

I cover my mouth I'm laughing so hard.

"You have a lovely laugh, Grace."

That stops me. I blush, looking down.

"And now you've stopped. I should have kept my mouth shut."

I feel like covering my face with a pillow. "Stop looking at me."

"Afraid I can't do that."

My eyes flick up to his. There he is, sitting on my bed, flirting with me. I have no idea what to do or say. His gaze is too much for me. I look down and nervously worry at one of my fingernails. What's wrong with me? Why can't I function around him? It's like being in high school all over again. God, I'm twenty-five years old. I assumed I'd figured out talking to the opposite sex by this point. Ryan looks at his watch and reaches to unwrap my knee. He shakes the ice-pack as he stands and pauses as if about to speak. Instead, he gives me a broad smile and wishes me sweet dreams on the way out.

I flex my knee, trying to see if a bruise is already forming or not, but it looked too blotchy from the ice. Getting settled to go to sleep, I think about Jon. Other than letting him know I had arrived safely, we have not had any contact. What is it going to be like when I get home? I only have three more days until I find out. Even though it had just been Jon in my thoughts, I fall asleep picturing Ryan's green eyes.

The next morning, my knee feels very sore and is a strange shade of purple. I slowly make my way to the kitchen to retrieve the ice pack. It's still early, and Kate is still asleep. I hope to ice my leg, shower, and be dressed for the day before she gets up. I don't even know if the ice is doing anything for my knee at this point but figure that it can't hurt. Afterward, while in the shower, I swear I can smell fresh coffee. Kate's up.

I wear a pair of yoga pants, happy the length covers my angry-looking bruise. Kate is pulling eggs out of the fridge when I walk into the kitchen. I impulsively walk over and give her a kiss on the cheek in greeting.

Kate's face breaks out into a wide grin. "Aren't you sweet? I was thinking eggs this morning. How do you like yours?"

I'm happy with any kind so she makes scrambled eggs

and tops them with shredded cheese. While she manages the eggs, I slice up a cantaloupe for us to share after pouring myself a cup of coffee. As we eat by the pool, Kate asks me if I would like to do any sightseeing. I am happy to go or stay at the house. she seems to want to take me to see the mermaid show at Weeki Wachee, which isn't far. I try to casually ask if Ryan will be coming. Kate doesn't say anything, but her eyes dance as she tells me that he has to work that day. I'm confused, wondering how we will get there.

"You can drive my car."

"You have a car?"

Kate had stopped driving a couple of years ago when she could not pass the eye exam to keep her license. She kept the car and just let Ryan drive it from time to time to make sure everything still worked. She knew it would make more sense to sell it but just couldn't part with it. She kept it stored at Ryan's house because he had a garage. She sends me over to his house with her spare key to collect it. I feel strange walking into Ryan's house alone, almost like I'm snooping. I have a valid reason for being there. Kate sent me to retrieve the car. It's just that once I'm there, I cannot help the compulsion to look around.

The front door opens into a sitting room similar to Kate's. The house in general seems the same only a mirror image, so the rooms are on different sides. Instead of a lanai, Ryan's rental has a garage. His style seems very minimalist, a beige sofa and TV in the front room, a bar-height dark wood table and chairs in the kitchen. I don't dare look in his bedroom. That would be crossing the line. I do look at the artwork he has on the walls, mainly black and white tropical photos. I wonder if they are pictures from his travels. The entrance to the garage is off the kitchen. As I pass the table, I notice a hoodie slung over the back of one of the chairs. I lift it to my nose. It smells like him. He wears a cologne I don't recognize but like. This smells like that mixed with a salty smell: the gulf or sweat, I wonder.

Once I'm in the garage, I stop to check out Kate's car. It's a silver Cadillac with a convertible top. I'm slightly intimidated driving it. Hopefully, this place isn't too far, and Kate still knows how to get there. I hit the button to open the garage door, and as slowly as possible, back Kate's Caddy out onto the street, swinging it around to pick her up. There's a garage door opener attached to the visor that I click to shut the door behind me. Weeki Wachee is an hour north from her house. As we drive, I ask her more about my mother. The one thing that still bothers me about Kate's version is I just can't picture my mom hanging on to anger that long to never let Kate back into her life.

Kate doesn't mince words. She accepts all the blame and feels like a part of her started pushing my mom away after Ronny died. After all of that time, once she understood my mother found someone to love her, my mother left and didn't look back. Kate doesn't blame her. She only wishes she could have understood better at the time the consequences of her actions. It still doesn't sit well with me, it just feels out of character for my mom to act that way. I have this image of her and have to accept the fact that maybe she is human and can hold a grudge. Kate seems bent on me not remembering my mother in anything less than a positive light.

"Grace, I'm not the same person I was those days. Living in that house, surrounded by all of those memories, was not healthy for me. I don't fault your mother for not forgiving me. I wasn't an easy person to be around. I was cold and angry and felt like I couldn't deal with the world around me."

I have a hard time connecting the image Kate portrays of herself with the person sitting next to me. I let it drop, not wanting to upset her. I have a good time seeing the mermaid show. The park is full of little girls and their parents or grandparents. I smile being able to lump myself into that category even though I'm much older.

Once we are back at Kate's house, she takes a nap while I return the car to Ryan's garage. Ryan is pulling into his driveway as I'm letting myself out of his house.

"We took Kate's car out," I explain, feeling my face get hot.

"Sorry, my place is a mess."

"What? It seemed clean, but I only saw the front room and the kitchen."

"No peeking at my boxers?"

"No, not that I would admit it if I had" I joke.

He rubs his chin and smiles "I will now assume you did."

"Don't!"

"But it's more fun that way. So what do you ladies have planned for lunch?"

"Kate's resting right now. I was just going to make myself a sandwich. Want one?"

Ryan follows me back to Kate's house and keeps me company in the kitchen while I make our lunch. He rambles on about his day. I like the sound of his chatter. We take our plates out by the pool. I'm really going to miss the weather. I'll not be outside like this until well into spring back home. Ryan pours us some lemonade and asks me how I like Kate's car. I tell him it's longer than any car I've ever driven so other than being nervous when I was parking I think it is a great car. Ryan loves that car, telling me how he would put the top down and drive Kate around town. It makes me wonder why Ryan seems content to spend his time with Kate instead of people closer to his own age.

I have been so distracted I miss what he asks me. "Sorry?"

"Want to go out with me tonight?"

"I don't know. What about Kate?"

"No worries. I cleared this with the boss lady last night."

"I guess."

"You don't have to if you don't want to."

"No. I didn't mean—what I meant to say was you don't have to."

"I know I don't have to, Grace. I'm asking you because I'd like to."

"Well, in that case..."

It is settled. Ryan will pick me up at seven. He helps me clear the plates before he goes back to work. Kate comes out not long after, having finished her nap. I'm onto her.

"Did you fake a nap so Ryan and I would be alone?"

"Oh, Ryan stopped by? How is he?"

"You can't fool me." I smile. "He's great and taking me out tonight."

"Oh, I'm so happy you said yes."

"Mm hmm. Has your matchmaking made you work up an appetite? Can I make you a sandwich?"

"Oh, that'd be lovely, dear."

That night, I wear a cream-colored sundress with little eyelets at the hem. The dress comes down to my knees. My bruise is an odd shade of blue now. I take a green cardigan with me in case it cools off. I wear brown ballet-style flats and a small, green crossbody bag for my wallet. I borrow Kate's curling iron, adding some gentle waves that hit just past my shoulders. As I put on some mascara, I wonder if all the sun has lightened my hair, or maybe I'm just not used to seeing it styled. Not one for much makeup, I actually put on a little blush. Pointless, I think, since I always seem to feel red-faced around Ryan.

"Do you think Ryan thinks this is a date, Kate?"

"I don't know, dear."

"Yes, you do."

She nods her head "Well, maybe."

"But I have a boyfriend."

"Then you really shouldn't be going on a date, dear."

"Kate!"

"I know Ryan will be here soon, but there was something I—"

"Knock, knock," Ryan calls out from the front room.

"Be right there," I call out. Then turning to Kate. "What were you saying?"

"It's not important. Come on, dear."

I follow Kate to the front room, stopping when I see Ryan. He's wearing khaki trousers and brown dock shoes with an untucked light blue dress shirt, his sleeves rolled to his elbows. His hair looks damp like he is fresh out of a shower.

Ryan gives Kate and me each a kiss on the cheek in greeting, murmuring, "You look lovely," to me as his mouth brushes my cheek.

"You too. I mean, you look great," I mumble.

"You kids have fun." Kate pushes us towards the door.

Ryan has just started the car when I turn to him. "This isn't a date."

He looks at me before moving his glance to the rear view mirror and backing out of the driveway. "Pity."

I cannot think of a response to that, so I just fold my hands in my lap and look out the window. We drive in silence until Ryan nears someplace called Ybor City. He takes me to a Cuban restaurant on 7th Avenue. It is dim inside, and there are a lot of people waiting for a table, but Ryan has a reservation so we are seated right away. While we look at the menu, I confess I have never had Cuban food before.

"Can't go wrong with arroz con pollo," Ryan suggests.

I think the Spanish-sounding dish sounds funny with Ryan's accent and ask him to say it again a couple of times before asking what it is. It sounds much more exotic than chicken and rice but something I'd like so when our server comes I order it. After dinner, we pop into a bar with a live band. I surprise Ryan by asking if he'd like to dance. The band plays cover songs of stuff I hear on the radio but with a beachy-sounding twist. Ryan is fun to dance with. He does not get too close but still takes my hands or rests his hands on my hips. I put my arms around his neck but the music stops for the band to take five.

Ryan leans his forehead on mine and breathes. "Why can't this be a date?"

I take a step back. What's the point? Even if this could be a date, I'm leaving in two days. There's no point getting all worked up over something that isn't going to happen. In the long run, I'll have to forget about Ryan. It's best to keep my distance. he gauges my reaction, and his face falls.

"Can I buy you a beer?"

He nods and follows me to the bar. The silence between us becomes uncomfortable.

Groaning, I try to lighten the mood. "Believe me. You

wouldn't want to be on a date with me. I'm awful, and noisy, and no fun. You really dodged a bullet."

He smiles at me and holds his glass up for cheers. "To dodging bullets."

"I'll drink to that," I smile, clinking my glass to his.

The rest of our evening is free of any awkward moments. We stroll along 7th Avenue, checking out the different shops, bars, and restaurants before turning back towards Ryan's car.

"Red punch buggy, no punch backs!"

"Ompf!" Ryan gapes at me "Did you just hit me?"

"Mm hmm."

"Why?"

"Have you ever played punch buggy?"

"'Fraid not."

"It's kinda hard in the dark." I cringe, thankful he can't see me as I feel my face redden.

"I'm listening." He chuckles.

"Oh hush. What I meant was it's harder to find punch buggies when it's dark out. That red one was a lucky call 'cause it was right in front of us."

"So how do you play?"

"See a bug, call it, punch, say no punch backs. That's about it."

"I don't want to play a game where I hit you."

"Well, you don't have to punch hard."

"You did."

"You looked like you could take it."

"Oh, I see how it is."

I just giggle, which makes Ryan shake his head at me. He drops me off in front of Kate's house.

"You're not coming in?"

"It's late. I have to get up early tomorrow. I have another fishing group going out."

"Oh, right. Well, thank you. I had a really great time."

"So did I."

"Will you be back in time for dinner tomorrow?"

"Should be."

"Oh, um, great. Okay. Bye."

The house is dark, and Kate has already gone to sleep. I change and get ready for bed. It takes me some time to fall asleep. I cannot help but think about how Ryan had wanted it to be a date. I wanted it to be a date too. I'm regretting telling him no. I try to think about Jon, try to picture his face, anything to not dwell on Ryan.

The smell of coffee wakes me the next morning. I head toward the kitchen. Kate is pouring herself a cup when I walk in.

"Morning, dear. Did you have fun last night?"

"Morning, Kate. Yes. I had a great time."

I set her coffee on a tray with some muffins and sliced cheese and follow her outside. I am really going to miss this weather.

I focus on my coffee. I'm not very hungry.

"Grace, there was something I wanted to ask you."

I look up from my cup "Yes?"

"You see, I've just enjoyed your stay so much, and I just wanted to let you know that if you'd like to I'd like for you to stay with me."

"What?" She wants me?

"Move to Florida, dear. I can tell you aren't happy in Ohio."

She has a point. I'm not.

"I can't." I argue even though part of me is rejoicing at the idea.

"Why not?" Her eyes soften.

"What about my job? Jon?"

"You wouldn't need to pay rent so you could take your time finding something."

"And Jon?"

"Only you can answer that question, dear" she says quietly.

"I just don't think I can."

"No matter what you decide, I just needed you to know that you're welcome to stay here as long as you like."

"That really means so much to me, and I will think about it. I just—I just don't know what to say."

I begin worrying at a muffin, pulling it apart and making more mess than eating it. Has my grandmother really just asked me to move to Florida? It sounds like a dream, but she's probably just being polite. She can't really mean it. But, if I stay, what will happen to Jon? There is no way he can afford the apartment without me. He could always get a studio. But what if he asks me to stay? Will he even ask me to stay? Kate reaches over and pats me on the hand.

"Is there anything you would like to do today, Grace?"

"I'm fine just hanging out around here."

"You had mentioned wanting to learn some of the meals I've cooked. Would you like to do that today?"

"That sounds great, but I have to warn you I'm a miserable cook."

"Oh hush, dear. I'm sure you're fine."

After eating, I clear the table and go to take a shower. I check my knee before getting in. It looks better than the night before. I dress in a pair of jeans and a short-sleeved sweater. I will be leaving the next day, I'm really having a hard time dealing with that, and now Kate asked me to stay. Why does the idea of it feel like I would be running away? And then there is Ryan to think of. He seems interested in me, but is it only because he knows I'm going away? I gather my dirty clothes together and look for Kate to see if I can do a load of laundry.

Kate is in the front room looking at old photos. I sit by her. She absentmindedly points people out, people I have never seen before: my great grandparents. There are also more pictures of my mother and my uncle Ronald. These photos are happier than the formal professional photo hanging in the hallway.

"Was Anne buried or cremated?"

I cringe at the thought of a mother having to ask that question about her own daughter. "Um, they were both cremated."

"Did you scatter their ashes?"

"Yes, in the Cuyahoga River back home."

"Is it a pretty river?"

"It used to be polluted but it's better now. It's very curvy. Mom loved it."

"Maybe someday I'll come visit you to see it."

"I'd really like that, Kate."

When we are done looking at the album, I ask Kate if I can use her washer and dryer. She tells me I'm silly to even ask and shows me where they are and how to work them. I hurry back to my room to grab my clothes, figuring it is safe to wash them all together as long as I set it on cold. Kate is making a chef salad in the kitchen when I find her. After lunch, she sits on her wicker loveseat and knits while I go for a dip. I lounge in an armchair float and chat with Kate while she is busy with her knitting. She's making another shawl. This one is a mint shade and is more ribbed than diamond patterned.

"Have you always knitted?"

Kate looks down at the project in her hands. "I learned

from my mother when I was very young. It's very calming. I like to have my hands busy, and it feels nice to make the shawls for someone going through a rough patch. Your mother knew how to knit. Did she ever teach you?"

I shake my head.

"Oh."

After my swim, I change back into my jeans and sweater for my cooking lesson. We're making meatloaf. I remember hearing that some people use corn flakes in meatloaf, not Kate. She uses stuffing. The recipe is simple. Forming the loaf is a bit messy, but I'm certain once we glaze it this is something I can probably make on my own. We go back onto the lanai once the meatloaf is in the oven.

"Would you ever like to learn how to knit?"

"Maybe someday. Have you made anything other than shawls?"

"Here, come with me."

I follow Kate back into the house and to the second spare bedroom, this one smaller than the one I'm sleeping in. It's painted a light sage green, leaning more grey than green. There's a pine-framed daybed and matching dresser. In one corner, a wooden rocking chair that has been painted white sits next to a brass side table. Instead of paintings, there are pieces of stained glass hanging on the walls: a hummingbird, an orchid, and a geometric pattern. There is one piece hanging in front of the window: a frog, casting green and yellow hued shadows on the floor and bed. Kate opens the closet and begins pulling hanger after hanger down of knitted goods. Sweaters, scarves, a dress, cardigans, and cowl neck scarves.

"Did you make all of these?" I lift one sweater up off the daybed to look at the pattern on it. There are four different colors mixed together to create a row of flowers at the waist and wrists.

"I've been knitting a long time, dear. Now, mainly making shawls for the church."

"These are gorgeous."

"Would you like any?"

"I couldn't."

"No, please take whatever you'd like. I would like you to have something I made."

"Really?"

"Of course, dear." Kate lifts my hand in hers and gives it a squeeze.

I carefully look at each piece and settle on a blue sweater with white x marks at the waist and wrists, and after Kate's insistence, a purple and black cowl scarf as well.

"Thank you so much. I absolutely love them. I will think of you every time I wear either of them."

"Are you sure you can't stay?"

"Well, I wouldn't be able to wear these here, would I?" I try to joke, but the thought of leaving is really upsetting me.

We hang everything back up and the go back to sit by the pool. Once Kate is settled with her knitting again, I excuse myself to check my laundry. I purposely take my time pulling each item out one by one and placing them into the dryer. As though delaying this will somehow slow the movement of my last full day here. Once the dryer is going, I go back outside and sit in comfortable silence with Kate. I'm not sitting right next to her but am close enough to her that every so often she leans forward and pats me on the knee. It's nice, like a reminder that I am wanted.

I'm sure Kate wonders why I am so set on going home. I admitted I don't love Jon, so what's pulling me back? A sense of obligation? A fear of the unknown? I spend most of the afternoon second guessing myself. The buzz of the oven timer brings me back to reality. I tell Kate to sit and go to take the loaf out of the oven. I'm holding it with mitts when I hear Ryan call out a greeting from the front door.

"Good God, that smells like heaven. Kate, you are truly trying to ruin me for all other women."

I have just set the pan onto the stovetop when Ryan pulls me into a hug. "Hullo, Grace."

Hugging him back, I can't help but giggle at his forwardness. "Hello, Ryan."

He loosens his grip a fraction, and I step out of it, trying not to think about how good he smells. I decide not to make the moment awkward by asking why he hugged me but instead just enjoy it. I prepare a plate for each of us while Ryan opens a bottle of wine. He helps me bring the food out, and we sit.

"I'd like to make a toast," Ryan says, lifting his glass. "To Grace, for—no pun intended—gracing us with her presence."

"Har har." I reply as we clink glasses.

"You'll come back and see us again, won't you?" Ryan asks, looking at Kate and then at me.

"I'd love to."

"I asked Grace to move in with me."

My mouth drops open. I'm surprised Kate mentioned it.

"That's great!" Ryan is beaming. "So will you do it?"

I start to reply, but Kate answers for me. "She said no, but I'm hoping she'll change her mind."

Ryan's face falls, and I suddenly feel like crying. Why does this feel like a mistake? A somber mood drifts over the rest of our meal. It's awful to imagine Ryan and Kate having dinner without me tomorrow. It's too much for me, and I excuse myself, half of my food uneaten. I flee to my room and sit on the edge of my bed, my mind reeling. The idea of going back to Ohio is becoming physically painful but to stay somehow seems to scare me even more. I'm not one to make rash decisions. Even agreeing to come to Florida in the first place had been out of my comfort zone. The idea of leaving my life in Ohio behind and moving to Florida is incomprehensible.

I raise my head at the sound of a knock on the door. I dry my eyes and stand before saying, “Come in.” It’s Ryan.

"What's going on Grace?"

"I'm being silly. Please don’t worry about me. I'm sorry for seeming like such a basket case."

"A basket case?"

I laugh, guessing they don’t have that term in New Zealand. "A crazy person."

"Oh, I don’t think you're crazy."

"Thank you, Maybe I just feel crazy."

"Would you like to talk about it?"

"Trust me. If I told you everything that's going through my mind right now, you would change your mind about the whole crazy part."

Ryan sits in the armchair, steepling his hands in front of him. "Try me."

I hesitate, and he cocks his head at me, so I take a deep breath and begin. "I'm scared of moving to Florida. I've lived in Ohio my whole life, and it's all I've ever known. Yes, I'm not happy there right now, but I have a boyfriend, and even though things are not good right now, moving here this way would feel like giving up. I don’t know if I'm ready to give up, and I have a good job. If I came down here, would I be able to find anything like that? I know Kate said I wouldn’t have to worry about money or anything but I just can't do that. I would feel like a mooch."

"Mooch?"

"Someone who takes without giving anything back."

"Sorry, thought you said pooch, like a dog. I misheard you. But, I don't think Kate would ever think that."

"But I would" I sigh.

He shrugs. "Fair enough. Carry on."

"So this whole idea is just making me feel crazy because I have no idea what to do. The idea of leaving is awful, but I feel like I can't just make a decision this big in a day."

"All very valid points, Grace. I'm sticking to my previous assessment that you're not crazy."

"So what do I do?"

"If it were up to me, I'd say stay but I'm partial to that outcome."

I blush and look at my hands. I'm nowhere closer to knowing what to do.

"Kate's worried she's upset you. Let's go back out and let her know you're having a little conflicted moment but it's all been settled." Ryan stands and reaches his hand out to me.

Taking it, I follow him back outside.

"I'm sorry if I'm becoming a pest," Kate says as soon as we're back outside.

"No, I'm sorry. It's all me." I lean down to give her a hug.

"And it's nothing another glass of wine won't cure," Ryan says as he tops off all of our glasses.

"Trying to get us drunk?" I joke.

"All part of my master plan." He makes a very poor attempt to waggle his eyebrows. "I will go fetch another bottle to allow you two to laugh at my expense in my absence."

When he walks into the kitchen, Kate and I look at

each other and dissolve into laughter. He looks extremely offended when he comes back and we are still laughing, which only causes us to laugh harder.

"I'm disappointed by this turn of events," he deadpans, taking a large drink of his wine.

At some point during the second bottle of wine, Ryan talks me into putting on my swimsuit as this might be my last opportunity to swim in the pool before I leave. Not having a valid argument to that, I go put it on, and we get into the pool.

I'm now feeling pretty tipsy. Ryan and I drape our arms over the edge and chat with Kate. We start a third bottle of wine not too long after that, but pleading exhaustion, Kate goes to bed, leaving us alone. I feel far too close to Ryan so I swim over to the other side of the pool. If Ryan can tell why, he doesn't say. He just turns so that his back is up against the pool wall as he faces me. The pool isn't very big so the distance I've put between us doesn't amount to much. He still feels too close, and with Kate gone and the wine, I feel shy and nervous.

I try not to look at him and turn my back to him, pretending to be very interested in the night sky. I tense when I hear water lapping the pool walls as he swims over to me.

He's behind me. "Grace."

It's almost a plea. I can't turn to look at him. "Yes?"

"Grace, would you look at me?"

I don't respond, and I don't turn around. I have a feeling that if I do, he will kiss me. After a few moments, he leans against the pool wall just next to me.

"I just want you to know I think you're lovely."

I keep my head forward but peek at him from the side. His arms are on the pool deck, one hand on top of the other with his forehead resting on top.

"I think you are lovely too, Ryan."

His head pops up, and he rests his chin on his hand. He's smiling. We stay like that for some time before I, like Kate, plead exhaustion. Ryan readies to leave, studying his shoes and telling me what time he'll come pick me up to take me to the airport. I stand in my towel, on the lanai, and watch him leave. I'm kicking myself for not turning around in the pool, but it's better this way. If he'd kissed me and it had been wonderful, it would be that much harder to go home. I lock the backdoor behind me and go to my room, pausing at the picture on the wall. I have become accustomed to seeing the faces from the photo before I go to bed.

I retrieve my cell phone from my room and snap a photo of the picture. It's not the same, but it will do. I snuggle into the most comfortable bed I've ever slept on for one last night of sleep.

Over indulgence of wine can result in sleeping in. Days when you must get on an airplane are stressful enough without feeling as though you are already behind. I wake up an hour later than I had planned. I rush to the dryer to retrieve my clothes and dump them on my bed before taking a shower. Once I'm dressed, I pack my clean clothes and go off in search of Kate. She's in the kitchen looking as though she is also suffering from the effects of too much wine. I'm relieved to see a fresh pot of coffee. Ryan had brought some croissants the day before and Kate has baking chocolate in the fridge, so I whip up a few chocolate croissants for us in the microwave. They're hot so while they cool I go off in search of some Advil to assist with the dull thud in my head. Kate is quiet over breakfast. I feel like it's my fault for not agreeing to stay. It's weird not knowing what to say to make her feel better.

I get up to clear the plates, and Kate stops me, putting her hand on my forearm. "Just know you still have family, Grace. I may be old, but we're all each other has left at this point. I want you to know that I love you and always will."

I sink down to my knees next to her and allow Kate to pull me into a hug. We're both crying, I suddenly feel overwhelmed by the idea that I'm not alone in the world. I had clung to Jon after my parents' deaths because of this. I'm not certain why Kate is crying, maybe it has something to do with my mother, maybe it is just because she will miss me. When we separate, Kate grabs a napkin to wipe my tears.

"Please know I've thought about staying. It's just not a choice I can make this quickly, but know that even though I'm going back to Ohio today, I've not decided against coming back."

"It would make me so happy."

"I just need time to think" I say lowering my head.

She runs her hand gently over my hair. "I understand, dear."

I stand and continue gathering our plates to clear the table. When I finish, I walk through each room of the house I spent time in to make sure I've not forgotten something. My bags are packed and standing at attention in the front room for when Ryan arrives. As I wait for him, I sit with Kate while she knits. She's now making a baby blanket for the daughter of a friend. It's cream-colored with a pink border. Watching her knit, I can suddenly picture my own identical baby blanket. I still have it in a box in my closet back home.

"You said my mother knew how to knit, right?"

"She did."

"I have a baby blanket like this back home." I gently touch a corner of the blanket.

"If your mother did not make it, there's a good chance that was a blanket I had made for her as a baby. I had one that I never knew what happened to it. If that's the same one, I'm happy to know she used it with you." Kate reaches out to pat me on the knee.

Ryan enters not long after. Kate flutters around me, wanting to make me a snack before I leave, but my stomach is unsettled from the night before and the thought of flying. I hope a bag of Chex Mix at the airport will help. When we hug goodbye, Kate clings to me. I can tell by the way Kate is breathing that she is near tears. I don't want to cry in front of Ryan again, but will have no choice if I see Kate cry. I give her a kiss on the cheek and release my arms. Kate walks us to the door, pulling me down to give me a kiss. Ryan pulls both of my suitcases and loads them into his Jeep while I double check my purse for my ticket and ID. Kate stands in the doorway, waving while I climb into Ryan's Jeep.

"And we're off," Ryan says, backing out.

"Thank you for taking me to the airport."

"We're going to miss you."

I can't tell him how much I am going to miss him as well without feeling silly so I nod and look out the window, feeling more depressed with each palm tree we pass. It doesn't take long to get to the airport. Ryan refuses my request to just drop me off and parks instead. I follow him to the airline counter, and he waits with me until my bag is checked. I'm waiting for him to leave, but he seems unable to. As we approach the security area, we both know he can't go any farther. Before I walk into the roped-off area, he pulls me into a hug. I rest my forehead on his neck, breathing him in.

Ryan's arms are so strong around me. I don't want him to let go, but he does. Just before his arms release me, he gently kisses the top of my head. I reach for his hand and give it a squeeze, then move into line. As I navigate the rope-lined path, I look back each time the line stops, and each time, Ryan is still there, watching me. When I reach the front of the line where I have to take off my shoes and put them and my carryon onto the conveyor belt, I look back one more time to wave and see he is gone.

Sad I'd not been able to see him one last time, I pass through security in a daze, only to be stopped because I have forgotten to take off my belt. The TSA agent takes it from me to have it through the scanner and makes me walk through the detector again. I apologize while putting my belt and shoes back on, then go to find my gate. I have a direct flight for the return, and Jon will pick me up from the airport. I take out my cell phone to text him a reminder of when my flight will be landing.

Time to get back to reality, I think to myself. Sure, Florida had been a nice break with kayaking and mermaids, but that is not my life. It's Saturday. I'll have all day tomorrow to get settled and ready to go back to work on Monday. This is my life. I just need to accept that.

When I land in Cleveland, I can't find Jon. I move out of the path of travelers and text him, asking if he is there. Jon replies that he will meet me at baggage claim. I'm not sure why that bothers me. Somehow, I had expected him to wait just past security. I tuck my phone into my purse and pull my coat out of my carryon suitcase. I'm still inside the airport but already freezing, wondering what the temperature is like outside. I see Jon right away as I enter the baggage claim area. He looks bored.

"Hi, Jon."

He makes no move to hug me. "How was Florida?"

"Good, thanks."

Silence.

Jon stands off to the side with my carryon while I wait for my suitcase to come around the carousel. Once I have it, I wheel it over to him, and he turns and begins making his way to the parking lot, pausing to put on a hat before walking outside. I cringe at the blast of cold air and grimace as I step into it and try to keep up with him. When we get to my car, Jon hands me the keys before going to sit in the passenger seat and leaving me to load my bags in the trunk. My fingers feel like icicles by the time I shut the trunk and climb into the car. I put the heat on high and blow on my hands as I rub them together.

Jon hands me the parking ticket and we leave, not having to pay since Jon had parked less than an hour. I wish he was driving but don't say anything about it.

"How was your week?" I ask.

"Fine."

Silence.

I turn on the radio to fill the void. When we get back to our apartment, Jon helps me carry the larger case up the stairs. He stays in the front room while I go to our bedroom to call Kate.

"I just wanted to let you know I made it home safe."

"Oh, thank you, dear. Did you have a good flight?"

"It was fine. Thank you."

"I miss you already, dear."

"I miss you too, Kate."

"Well, I hope you'll come back and see me again soon."

"I'll try."

When we end our call, I unpack my bag, happy that I don't have laundry to deal with. As I hang the sweater Kate knit, I decide I'll wear it the next day. When I'm finished putting my things away, I go to the kitchen to make a snack. There isn't much to eat. Jon is sitting in his chair watching me.

"I think I'll run to the store and pick some things up. Would you like to go with?"

"I'll stay here."

"Is there anything I can get for you?"

"I'm good."

I'm better dressed for the cold on this outing, hat and gloves on. I stop to get gas while I'm out so I won't have to do it the next day before going on to the store. I walk the aisles in a daze, randomly filling my cart. I pick up ground beef and stuffing to make for dinner Sunday. It seems like everything I'm getting I had eaten at Kate's: a cantaloupe, muffins, eggs, and wine. Will eating the same foods make me feel like I'm still with them? I pick up more food than I had intended and have to make three trips from the car up the stairs to bring it all up. Even Jon seems surprised by the amount of food as he gets up to help me unload.

"Wine?"

"Why not? Want to open it and have a glass with me?"

Jon's brows come together above the bridge of his nose before he pulls a bottle opener out of one of the kitchen drawers. Our wine glasses are a bit dusty, from lack of use. Jon rinses and dries them before he pours us a glass.

I lift my glass and motion for Jon to lift his as well. "To home."

He hesitates before touching his glass to mine and taking a drink.

I'd pick up an easy skillet meal for two out of the frozen section of the store. It's an Italian chicken dish. It's a bit early for dinner but not by much, so I go ahead and make it since I'm hungry. While it's cooking, I steam a bag of frozen broccoli in the microwave. I smile when Jon puts plates out on the table. When dinner is ready, we sit together and eat. Jon gets up during our meal to refill our glasses. Maybe this can work.

The wine goes to my head, and I go to bed earlier than normal. Part of me is disappointed when Jon makes no move to follow me. As I drift to sleep, I mourn the loss of Kate's comfortable bed and I wonder if Kate and Ryan are still up, sitting by the pool. My last thought before sleep overtakes me is if they are missing me as well.

The next morning when I wake, it takes me a moment to figure out where I am. I turn my head to see Jon quietly sleeping beside me. After looking at the time on my phone, I decide there is no point trying to fall back asleep. I wander out to the kitchen and make a cup of coffee before warming up a muffin in the microwave and coating it with butter. I take my muffin and coffee over to the table and slowly nibble it and sip my coffee while they cool. Wanting some fruit I get up and am slicing a cantaloupe in half when Jon walks out. He nods in my direction, pours himself a cup of coffee and sits in his armchair.

"Is there anything you needed to do today?"

He pauses for a beat to consider my question, then shakes his head and turns on the TV. I take my cantaloupe and sit back down at the table, my back to him. I pinch my eyes shut as I try not to let my hopes fall. Is this what it's going to be like between us? I'd hoped that my absence would in some way make Jon miss me. If Jon had missed me, he isn't showing it. I can't help but wonder what he's thinking. Is he even happy?

I slowly dig my spoon into the flesh of the fruit, my knuckles hitting the inside of the bowl I had made with its rind. My mind drifts to Ryan, to the feel of his arms around me as he said goodbye. I can still picture him as he stood in the airport to greet me that first day. I turn back to look at Jon as he watches TV. Now that he was working again, I'd hoped he would come out of whatever funk he seemed to be in.

Steeling myself, I get up and go sit closer to him on the sofa. "I think we should talk."

He mutes the TV. "About?"

I take a deep breath "Us."

"I'm listening."

"It feels like we don't talk anymore."

He shrugs "We're talking right now."

"It didn't use to be like this."

"Like what?"

I close my eyes."It just feels like you don't even like me."

"I do."

"Do you?" I blush, opening my eyes. "You haven't even touched me since I've been home."

Jon looks down at his hands.

"My grandmother asked me to move to Florida."

He hesitates "Are you?"

"I'm thinking about it."

His eyes search mine "What's stopping you?"

"You. Us."

He pauses "I think you should go" he says then looks away.

I struggle to take a breath. It feels like my lungs are burning. "You don't want me to stay?"

He doesn't respond, just turns back to the TV and unmutes it. My mouth drops as I process what has just happened. That's it? That is what I have been waiting to hear all of this time? I stand, pulling the belt of my robe snug around my waist as I slowly walk back to our bedroom to lie down. I pull Jon's pillow to my chest and breathe in his scent. He thinks I should go. He had not even followed me knowing I was upset. He is lost to me. My Jon who had loved me is gone. I unplug my phone from the charger and call Kate.

"Kate?"

"Grace, are you alright?"

"I'll move to Florida."

"What happened? Are you alright?"

I'm crying and not able to reply right away. I can hear Ryan in the background and then some shuffling as I picture Kate handing him the phone.

"Grace?"

"I'm here."

"You sound like you're crying. Is everything okay?"

"I think Jon just broke up with me."

"Fucking idiot."

I hear him cover the speaker and say something to Kate.

"Kate says you'll move down."

"Mm hmm."

"Right away?"

"I have to call my boss and see if Jon can take over the lease. It renews next month. Maybe we'll both just move out."

"Kate wants to know if you're all right staying there in the mean time."

I rest my head on my hand "I guess. Part of me wishes I never came back."

"Everything's going to be okay. Kate and I are here to help you."

I look up and see Jon leaning on the doorframe.

"I need to go."

"Well, call back after you talk to your boss."

"Okay. Bye."

"So you're going to go?" Jon asks.

I nod, setting my phone on the bedside table.

"Was that your grandmother?"

"Yes."

We speak for a few minutes. Jon doesn't think he can afford the place by himself and wants to see if I will still pay my share of the bills the last month even if I'm not there. Money. That's what he had been concerned about. I have no desire to fight and agree. Before he leaves, he tells me he will start sleeping on the couch. That makes sense; no reason to still share a bed. After he goes back into the front room, I pull my knees up into my chest and rock back and forth slowly. My mind is telling me I should be crying but no tears come. It's more of a "what just happened?" feeling. I'm scared I don't know how to be around him for the next two weeks. I want to say I feel relieved but I don't. If anything, I feel numb.

I pull out my laptop and type an email to my manager explaining that my grandmother has asked me to move to Florida, and since she is my last remaining relative, I feel it is something that I should do and that I need to give my two weeks' notice. The email address is my boss's personal email so I'm not surprised when my phone starts ringing thirty minutes later. I have worked in that doctor's office longer than I have dated Jon. My manager is worried I'm making a rash decision and is calling more as a friend than an employer.

We talk for over an hour. I tell her all about Florida and my grandmother. I tell her about learning I had an uncle and how he had died. It's when I talk about Kate and the relationship we're forming that Kim, my manager, gets it. Kim had been there for me after the deaths of my parents, and while she doesn't know everything that has been going on with Jon, she suspected something was wrong. When I tell her that Jon told me I should go Kim isn't surprised. Kim admits that during the time Jon had been unemployed she had almost told me to kick him out. The one thing I don't tell Kim about is Ryan. It feels like it will take something away from moving close to be with family if I admit I also have a crush on my grandmother's hot neighbor.

Kim is sad that I'm leaving but accepts my notice, saying that she will put together an office going away party for me. I feel a weight lifted knowing that I won't be leaving my office awkwardly. I've worked there almost four years. I'll not miss flu season, but I will miss my coworkers, especially Kim and Nikita. I ask Kim not to say anything until I tell Nikita myself. Kim agrees and says once Nikita knows she will send an email out to the office. I have to laugh when Kim starts saying she's going to miss me. I remind her that I've not left yet.

When I hang up, I walk to the kitchen, suddenly hungry. Jon is on his cell phone when I come out. He sees me then puts on his coat to finish his call outside. That's another thing we'll have to figure out, I think, annoyed he feels he has to leave the room to talk to someone. He's on my phone plan. I have been thinking about changing providers anyway because I don't want to deal with having to share data, and our phones are already out of contract. I make myself a sandwich and wait for Jon to come back in. When he does, I tell him I'll be turning off our phones before I leave. Jon replies that he had figured as much and says a friend is on his way to pick him up.

"Will you be back by dinner?"

"Probably not."

Jon takes a shower and gets dressed so he can be ready

to go. Where, I don't know. It's not my business to know where he goes anymore. After he leaves, I decide I want to make the meatloaf anyway. I can eat the leftovers at work, and it will remind me of Florida. Once it's in the oven, I call my grandmother back. Something about her phone makes it hard for Kate to hear me. Kate asks if it would be alright if I call Ryan instead, and he can relay the message. She gives me his number. Considering Kate can't hear me, I don't really have a choice and call Ryan.

"Hullo?"

"Hi, Ryan. It's Grace. Kate can't hear me, so she asked that I call you."

"Your grandmother needs a hearing aid for the telephone, but she won't listen to me."

"Sorry about that. Why won't she get one?"

"She's stubborn and thinks they look funny in people's ears."

I'm not sure why I think that's so funny, but it makes me laugh. I tell Ryan about the conversation I had with my boss. Ryan is happy for me that it had gone as well as it had. I have two weeks to pack up my life here and move. The idea is daunting. My first thought is to drive, but I'm scared to. It's over one thousand miles from Cleveland to Tampa. There's no way I can do that in a day. I probably can't even do it in two days. That means having to stay somewhere, by myself, along the way.

"What if I flew up and drove down with you?"

Depression

a state of feeling sad
-Merriam Webster

It's settled. Ryan buys a ticket to Cleveland. My last day of work is Friday, and Ryan is flying in that evening. Jon has already moved out, taking most of our furniture with him. I was especially happy to see his armchair go, I could only see what I had lost when I looked at it. Besides, I don't need any of it where I'm going. I do, however, keep the TV and laptop in exchange. Jon moved in with a coworker who already had a TV so he is fine with it. I buy an air mattress to sleep on once he leaves. It's strange coming home to such an empty house. I'm partly relieved. This way I will be able to turn the keys over to the complex manager without any worry Jon will do something to screw up us getting our deposit back. Jon said I can keep it.

I make multiple trips over those two weeks to Goodwill to donate things I no longer need, like winter coats and snow boots. I keep one good coat and work hard to purge other unneeded things. I'm nervous about Ryan coming and spending the night, and the fact that we will be sharing hotel rooms on the way down to Tampa. He said he has no problem sleeping on my floor that first night, but it's going to be weird.

Even after all of my purging, I'm worried not everything will fit in my car. Ryan promises that his packing skills are legendary. I hope he's right. On my last day of work, they have a luncheon in my honor. Kim, awesome boss that she is, lets me cut out early afterward. Nikita sniffles as she walks me to my car.

"You're still coming over tomorrow morning, right?"

"Yes. I just can't believe we don't work together anymore."

I haven't said anything about Ryan being gorgeous. Nikita only knows a friend of my grandmother is flying up to help me with the move, but that is all. I'm looking forward to seeing Nikita's reaction when she sees Ryan.

"I know. Feels really weird being unemployed," I grimace, still feeling a bit crazy for leaving a good job."You'll find something in no time. Besides, I saw the letter of recommendation Kim wrote for you. Any place that reads it would be crazy not to hire you."

"It really sucked saying goodbye to her."

"Is she coming by tomorrow too?"

"She can't."

"Alright. Give me a hug."

I give Nikita a hug and head home. As I cross the river, I tear up a little bit, saying goodbye to my parents. Since Kim let me leave early, I have enough time to change out of my scrubs and straighten the apartment up a bit before I have to go get Ryan. I feel silly organizing the crates and bags, wondering why I am wasting my time trying to organize a pile. Getting antsy, I leave for the airport. I'm thirty minutes early and circle the parking lot a few times, wanting to find a good spot. Ryan is in for a rude awakening weather wise. It's very cold and sleeting. I have an extra hat in my pocket for him, if he needs it.

He hadn't planned on bringing much, knowing that space in my car will be at a premium. I manage to nab a great spot near an entrance. I check my hair and makeup before getting out of the car. The gesture, at least for my hair, ends up being pointless since I put my hood up once I'm out of the car. Going to stand by the security checkpoint, I check Ryan's flight to see if it is still on time.

I lean up against a wall and fidget as I watch passengers filing out in all directions. I try to look at every face as they pass, but there are way more of them than there are of me. Ryan sees me first.

"Hullo!"

I look around, trying to place where his greeting is coming from when he's suddenly right in front of me, pulling me into a hug.

"Well, you're a sight for sore eyes."

I laugh. "Long flight?

Ryan nods, not letting me go. I swat him on the arm. "Can I take you out for a burger?"

He just nods and grins down at me. Ryan only has a small duffle bag so we head straight to my car. Before we get outside, I stop him to see if he's brought a hat. He hasn't and is touched when I pull out a beanie for him. Once he has it on, I have to admit it looks pretty good on him. Seeing Ryan's reaction to the cold, I hurry to my car and get the heater going.

"Grace, why does my ass feel like it's burning?"

"Oh, sorry. I turned on the seat heaters." I reach over to switch his to low.

"Next time warn a fella."

"Will do" I laugh, trying not to think about his ass.

"So where're you taking me?"

"To Swensons. Awesome burger, but it's a drive in. Do you want to eat there or bring the food back to my place?"

"Can we take it back to your place?"

Once we have our food, I drive home. It's weird to think that after tomorrow I won't be able to call it that anymore. I warn him to watch his step on the way up the stairs. Ryan does fine. I slip twice. Damn stairs. Once inside, I give him a quick tour: pile of stuff, empty room, empty room, air mattress, kitchen, and bathroom. Ryan laughs at my descriptions, and after setting his bag down, goes to the bathroom. I unpack our food onto the kitchen counter, grab a roll of paper towels, and make a picnic for us in front of the TV. I am switching on the news to get the next day's weather when Ryan walks out.

He pulls off his beanie as he walks into the front room, making his hair go crazy. He looks at me in confusion as I bring my hand up to my mouth to keep from laughing. Walking over I finger comb his hair back down as he looks down at me. Whoa. I take a step back, almost knocking over my drink to put some space back between us. Ryan notices my reaction and gives me a half smile as he sits down to eat.

I turn the volume up so I can hear the weather forecast. It will be cold but clear the next day. Our goal, depending on how long it takes to get everything in my car and do the final walk through of the apartment, is to get to West Virginia, maybe even Virginia, that day. I sit, turning the volume back down.

"You like?" I ask Ryan between bites.

His mouth is full so he nods enthusiastically while I snag another onion ring.

"Does Kate have a grill?"

Ryan finishes the bite he is chewing before answering. "She does."

"We should make burgers one night."

"Great idea. Maybe we'll even get artichokes for you to put on top."

I blush, happy that he remembers. After we eat, he calls Kate to let her know he arrived safely, well best he can. He shakes his head when he hangs up the phone mumbling something about her needing a hearing aid. We watch TV until I suggest we get some sleep before the long day ahead. I bring out one of the pillows from my room and an old sleeping bag for Ryan to use.

"Are you sure you don't want the air mattress? I feel awful making you sleep on the floor."

He shakes his head. "Don't worry, Grace. One night won't hurt me. I'll just pretend I'm camping."

"Do you like to camp?"

"I do, but I like most outdoor activities. You?"

"It's been a while. I used to camp with my dad."

After we trade goodnights I go to bed. I take forever to fall asleep, my stomach in knots as I think about leaving everything I've ever known. I wake before my alarm, Ryan is still sleeping so I shower. Refreshed, I step out wrapped in a towel, startled to find Ryan standing at the door.

"Bah!"

"Whoa, um, sorry. Didn't mean to scare you. Just, well, nature calls."

"Of course. Right. I'm sorry." I keep a tight grip on my towel as I brush past Ryan on the way to my bedroom. I notice he takes his time going into the bathroom and shutting the door for someone who has to go. I get dressed and drape my towel over the now empty rod in my closet, hoping it will be dry enough to pack in an hour or so. I pack a small bag of items that I'll need changes of clothes, most of my toiletries, and cell phone charger. This bag and Ryan's duffle will be the last items we pack. I leave my hair down to dry and unplug the stopper from the mattress so it can deflate before walking into the front room.

Ryan is looking out the window into the courtyard, stretching with his arms over his head. It makes his shirt lift up as well so I see the waistband of his briefs and some of his tanned back. As though he can sense me, Ryan turns. I flush and look at my toes, wiggling them for good measure. Locating socks had been my plan when I walked out into the front room. Finding where I packed them, I pull a thick pair to go under my boots and two pairs to go in my duffle. We both turn when there is a knock on the door.

"That'll be Nikita. I hope you like bagels."

I pull open the door, and am surprised to see it's Jon, not Nikita, who stands there.

"Jon."

"Hi, Grace." He stops when he sees Ryan in the room behind me. He looks at me and then at Ryan again before continuing. "I wanted to see you before you left."

"Did you want to come in?"

"If you're busy I can take off."

"No, not at all. Come in. Jon, this is Ryan. He's a friend of my grandmother's."

Ryan tips his head in Jon's direction and then turns to me "Should I go roll up the air mattress?"

Jon's eyes widen. What is he thinking? "Um, sure. That'd be great. Thanks."

Once Ryan leaves the room, Jon asks. "Did he sleep here?"

"Yeah. He's driving down with me to Florida."

He looks like he is going to say something but turns and seems intent on examining the light switch.

"So how's the new place?"

"I miss you."

What? I stare at him. "But you said—"

Before he can answer, there is a loud boom at the door. I hurry to open it and find Nikita with her arms full.

"Did you kick the door?" I ask, taking the cardboard coffee carrier from her.

"No hands."

"Okay, well, thanks for coming. It is so sweet of you to help and to bring breakfast."

"No worries. I got a bunch of bagels so you all don't have to stop for lunch if you don't want to."

"Do I smell coffee?" Ryan walks out from my bedroom, and Nikita's mouth drops open. Jon notices her reaction and walks over to the window.

"Yep. This is Nikita. She brought coffee and bagels."

"Hi, Nikita. I'm Ryan, a friend of Grace's."

Jon stiffens when he hears Ryan say that he is my friend and not my grandmother's.

"Well, why don't you and Nikita each grab a bagel? I'm just going to talk with Jon. Um, Jon did you want to…" I motion towards our old room.

Jon hesitates but follows me, I turn back to see Ryan watching us before I walk into the room. Jon shuts the door behind him. The room is basically empty, except for the rolled up air mattress and the bedding that had been on it. I walk over to the room's one window and lean on the sill. Jon leans against the door and looks up at the ceiling.

"It feels weird that you're leaving."

"It feels weird for me too."

"Part of me doesn't want you to go."

Part of you? I close my eyes in an attempt to aid my mind in processing what he has just said.

"I know I told you that you should go, and I still think you should. You have family there. I'll just miss you."

I blink my eyes before a tear can escape. I want to speak but don't trust my voice. Instead, I curl my fingers into a fist and bring my hand to rest on my mouth while I compose myself. When my eyes open, I know that Jon is watching me, waiting for me to respond."I didn't think you cared anymore." I'm unable to keep my voice from breaking at the end.

Jon hurries over to me and pulls me into a familiar, though long absent, hug.

"I'll always care about you, Grace."

I nod my head against his chest.

"I just wanted to come tell you that." He slowly releases me, gently wiping a stray tear from my cheek.

"That means so much to me."

"So that guy?" He nods toward the door.

"Ryan?"

He looks at the floor. "Are you two?"

"What? No" I say quickly, too quickly.

Jon looks at me like there is something else he wants to say before turning toward the door. "I should go."

"You don't have to."

"I don't want to get in the way. Will you call me, when you get to Florida?"

I don't know what else to say. "I can do that."

I walk him to the front room, giving him one last hug before he leaves. Afterward, when I turn to face Ryan and Nikita, I notice their expressions. Ryan looks wary, like he isn't sure what to do and Nikita looks concerned, worried Jon's visit may have upset me.

"Have you guys eaten yet?"

They both nod and I help myself to a cinnamon raisin bagel with cream cheese. Holding half of my bagel in one hand, I grab a small box and head towards my car, taking bites as I make my way down the stairs. My car keys are in my pocket so I inhale the rest of my bagel to grab them. I pop the trunk and set the box inside. Ryan and Nikita are right behind me with more boxes. We are able to fill every single spare inch of space in my trunk before moving on to the back seat. The TV goes in first, its screen facing the backseat, and boxes and bags stacked behind it. The last couple of boxes and our duffle bags prove to be somewhat of an issue.

One bag eventually ends up in the foot area of the front passenger seat, and the other rests on top of the middle console. As Nikita and Ryan do a final sweep, I walk over to the leasing office to get someone to do a final walk through. The extra leasing agent is showing an apartment so I have to wait a couple minutes before someone can help me. When I get back to the apartment, I see Nikita and Ryan trying to figure out how to fit the rolled up air mattress in the car.

"Don't worry about it. Nikita, do you want it? If you don't, we can just toss it."

"I don't really need an air mattress," Nikita says, crinkling her nose.

"I could use one," the leasing agent ventures.

I think about it for a moment. "If I pass the walk through, you can have it."

"Well, let's take a look."

I follow the leasing agent through each room. I'm not worried about her finding anything wrong. It's not like Jon or I had put any holes in the walls or stained the carpet. Once the inspection is complete, and I'm given my carbon copy of no issues found form I hand the air mattress over. Then Nikita surprises me by getting teary again.

"I'm gonna miss you, Grace." Nikita pulls me into a hug.

"You'll have to come down and visit me then."

"Can we go to Disney?"

"Um, sure."

Nikita leaves not long after that, and Ryan and I hit the road. I drive the first leg, since I'm familiar with the area. We're starting later than expected, with Jon stopping by and me having to wait for a leasing agent. Where we stop that night depends on how traffic is and how many stops we make. We're only on the road an hour before we make our first stop. I'm now regretting that cup of coffee. We go ahead and eat lunch while we're stopped to avoid another. Ryan asks about Jon.

I look away. "Jon just wanted to say goodbye."

"He seemed upset."

"He said he would miss me."

"That was nice of him to say."

He sounded so sincere. I look at him, and he shrugs. I wonder why he seems so interested in Jon. I change the subject and ask him about his business and who's managing it while he's gone.

"I've got a couple of longtime guys that can handle everything for a couple of days."

"It's just so cool of you to do this. Seriously, thank you."

"Anytime, Grace, really."

I believe him. When we get back into the car, Ryan takes a turn driving. One thing we learn on our journey is we don't like the same music. Ryan is a fan of hard rock. Me? More pop and emo. Compromising, we alternate stations every so often. While Ryan is driving I think more about what Jon said. I'm having a hard time processing his surprise visit, and since we left, this is really my first opportunity to think about it. Am I making a mistake going to Florida?

I'd been with him for three years. It's impossible to not feel a sense of loss at our separation. I wonder if things could have been different if I'd stayed. I have a habit of obsessing over what ifs. The more I think about it, the more depressed I become. I'm so distracted I don't realize Ryan has been talking to me.

"Grace?"

"Huh?" I glance at him.

"I just asked if you thought we should stop at the next rest area. A sign we passed said it would be the last one for some time."

"Uh, sorry. Sure, I guess that would be a good idea. It would be nice to stretch my legs."

"You okay?"

"Yeah, just zoned off there for a bit. Sorry."

"No need to apologize" he says, reassuring me.

Ryan moves over to the right hand lane in preparation for the upcoming turn off. I stare out the window, seeing Ryan's glances from the corner of my eye. I keep my head forward, and he frowns. I decide to stop thinking about Jon. It's clear it's affecting my mood and that he can sense it. Plastering a somewhat false smile to my face, I tell him after our stop we should play the license plate game. Ryan has never heard of it so while he takes the exit and parks I explain the rules to him.

"I have to warn you I'm very good at this game," I say competitively.

"At least there's no punching in this game, and maybe I'll have beginner's luck."

"Doubtful" I beam.

His mouth drops, and I laugh as I head to the ladies' restroom. When we meet back at the car, he asks if I want a snack or drink before we leave.

"Nah. Traffic isn't bad so let's try and see if we can make it to Virginia before dinner."

"You just want to start your game."

"Maybe."

"Cheeky thing, aren't you?" He grins.

I stick my tongue out at him and get into the car, then grab a sheet of paper from my purse and make a column for each of us. Ryan tries to call out cars from the parking lot, but I tell him to focus on getting out without hitting anyone and we will start once we are back on the freeway. By West Virginia, I have a substantial lead, and he glances over often at the sheet and shakes his head.

"I will now call you eagle eye. Really. Do you see better than 20 /20?"

"Hmm, I'm not sure. It's been a long time since I've seen an eye doctor."

"But you work in a doctor's office. Don't they do eye exams?"

"I'm sure I have a short one during my annual check ups, but I don't remember anyone ever making a big deal about my vision so I think your eagle eye theory is lacking, buddy."

"I'm only saying this because I used to always have vision problems. Last year, I finally got Lasik. Life changing."

"How so?"

"I had to find my glasses to see the alarm clock right next to my bed."

My mouth drops. "Yikes. That's bad. I can't picture you with glasses."

"I wore contacts a lot. Hated them."

"I've heard they can be irritating." I think about Jon and how he used to complain about his.

"If you want to see a picture of me with glasses, you can look in my wallet" his wallet is sitting in one of the drink holders.

"I'm not going to look through—NEVADA!—your wallet."

"Shit, another one. Grace, seriously. It's sitting right there. Besides, if you're distracted, I may catch up in this infuriating game."

"You've got two chances, slim and none. And we over-took slim a while back."

Ryan rolls his eyes but laughs and I grin as I reach for his wallet. It's a worn, brown leather tri-fold. Flipping it open, I can only see the top of his license and pull it out. Ryan looks younger with his glasses. They are small, wire-rimmed ones and make him look very studious.

"You looked so cute" I giggle.

"Looked? I'm not cute anymore?"

I copy Ryan's eye roll from a moment ago, trying not to blush and put his license back into his wallet. "Yes, you are still very cute."

"You think I'm cute?"

"Vermont!"

"You didn't answer my question."

"Not going to either."

"Aw, you're no fun."

"Yep, that's me. No fun at all." I blush, realizing I'm flirting with him. Guilt coils in my stomach as I think of Jon.

We make it to Virginia before dinner. Pulling off the highway in a small town, we pick up some fast food and check into a motel room. It's a surprise to the clerk when I ask for two double beds.

The clerk, who is an older woman, takes a second look at Ryan. "You sure?"

"Yes, thank you." I grumble, handing over my credit card as Ryan tries unsuccessfully not to laugh. He manages to keep it to a chuckle, which I appreciate. We walk out to the car and park it as close to our room as possible. I feel uncomfortable having all of my earthly possessions sitting in it while in an unfamiliar place. I beep the alarm three times before leaving it. The room in general isn't bad, just seems outdated. It appears to be clean, though, and that is all I care about. Ryan is adamant about having the bed closer to the door.

He makes such a big deal about it, I ask why.

"Well, to protect you should something happen."

It takes me a moment to respond. It feels like I have never known someone to be selfless. "You don't have to protect me."

"I know that."

"It's nice that you want to. Thank you."

Ryan furrows his brows and looks at me before calling Kate to let her know we were stopping for the night. I set my bag on the other bed and then sit at the small table to eat my burger. It's weird. I slept in the same apartment as him last night, but now we'll be sleeping in the same room, it feels more…personal. He'll be able to see me while I'm asleep. What if I snore? And the room in general isn't very big…What if I got gas? I cringe at the thought. I'm attracted to Ryan. The very fact that I am acknowledging that makes me feel guilty, like I have not properly dealt with my break up with Jon. Thinking of Jon and what he said confuses me.

If he'd only shown some semblance of affection towards me since my return from Florida, I would have never considered leaving. I loved him for three years. It's hard to turn off those reflexive emotions to him. The last year had been difficult, but when you care about someone it takes more than just a rough patch to give up. For me, it had been him telling me I should go. How could I stay and try to work things out if he wouldn't? But after this morning...

Ryan switches on the TV and begins flipping through the channels. He stops and looks to me for input. I'm not much help. I'm worn out, both physically and mentally. My plan after finishing my dinner is to get ready for bed. I'm sure the noise of the TV won't disturb me so I tell Ryan to pick whatever he likes. He looks bummed that I'm tired but doesn't say anything about it directly. He seems to be ignoring how tired he is himself, yawning frequently. I change into PJs in the bathroom and brush my teeth. I gaze enviously at the somewhat deep tub. The tub is a surprise given the age of the motel.

I wish I could take a bath and soak, but one of two things stops me. One: it would be weird to be naked one room over from him, and/or two, I am so tired I would probably fall asleep in it. I go back into the main room and get into bed. I turn so my back is to Ryan and don't even remember falling asleep. The next morning, I wake up to the sound of the shower going. I look at the alarm clock and am shocked to see it's already after eight. I have slept soundly for almost twelve hours. I've also not gone to the bathroom in all that time, and the sound of the shower is not helping.

I try to block the splashing sound of the shower out of my mind. At one point, I contemplate just going in there, but luckily, I hear the shower switch off. I climb out of bed and walk-dance to the door of the bathroom. I can hear Ryan on the other side, moving around. What is he doing? Giving up, I knock on the door.

"Yeah?"

"I, um, really have to, you know."

"Oh, right. Sorry."

He opens the door and moves past me. It is hard to not

stop and stare at him, damp, towel wrapped around his waist. I have little choice, though, and dash inside. When I'm done, I notice he has laid out his clothes for the day on the sink counter, meaning he is probably waiting, by the door, in a towel. I hurry out, thanking him. He's standing in the center of the room, between the beds, remote in hand. He turns and smiles, telling me it's no bother. I try not to stare, I do, but he's right there. In a towel. He stops when he finds a news channel and goes back to the bathroom to get dressed.

I retrieve my outfit for the day from my duffle, and once he comes back out of the bathroom, go to take my shower. The motel has crappy water pressure. Considering how weak the stream is, I'm amazed I heard Ryan's shower at all. Because of it, I take a longer than normal shower, just in the hopes of rinsing all of my conditioner from my hair. After showering, I dress in a pair of slouchy jeans and a baseball-styled, long-sleeved t-shirt. I put moisturizer on my face and skip makeup, but since it's cold out, I use the dryer attached to the wall to blow dry my hair. Not sure what our breakfast plans are, I go ahead and brush my teeth before going back out into the room. Ryan is staring intently at his phone with a print out of our map next to him.

"Everything okay?"

"Looking for a detour. There was a pileup on the road we should be taking. They showed a picture of it on the news. Trailer truck spilled its load. Looks like it will be a mess to clean up. I think it'd be best to avoid it all together."

"Good thing you watched the news. Are there any good alternate routes?"

"I found a couple that look promising. Just trying to figure out which is best."

"I'll leave that to you, I'm directionally challenged."

He looks up at me and raises a brow "Not the person to trust the compass with then?"

"Nope. The compass will cease being operational in my hands."

He shakes his head. "You can't be that bad."

"Maybe. I haven't really ventured outside of my normal routine in so long. But enough talk about that. What do you want to do for breakfast?"

"I saw a pancake place on the way in. Sound good?"

"Works for me."

I gather my things and double-check the bathroom before following Ryan out to the car. He's driving since he knows where we're going, I wait for him in the car while he goes to check out. At the restaurant, I order an omelet and Ryan a breakfast steak meal. When our food comes out, we both do a double take at the size of Ryan's plate. The amount of food on it can easily feed four people. He does his best but is about halfway when he gives up. Ryan pays for the meal since I paid for the motel room.

We're back on the road not long after. Ryan's alternate route takes us thirty minutes out of the way. Given the accident still has the other road blocked, it was a smart move. Even though I had slept so long the night before, the car and the uncongested highway lull me back to sleep. I jump when Ryan shakes my shoulder. Looking around, blinking rapidly, I realize we're at a rest stop.

"Thought it would be a good time for a stop. Sorry to wake you, but I wanted to see if you'd like to get out and stretch your legs"

"Oh, how long was I out?"

"About three hours."

"Really? I don't get why I'm so tired."

"I've heard moving can be emotionally draining."

"That must be it."

"Did you want to get out?"

"Yes, thanks"

I unfold myself from the passenger seat. It feels wonderful to stretch. I slowly walk around to the back of the car and lean on the trunk, looking about. The rest stop is on the small side. It has a gas station with a built in deli and a bank of vending machines near the bathrooms. There is a grassy area with a couple of picnic benches for people to sit and eat at. It's almost lunch time. I wonder if Ryan's hungry. He's gone to the restroom. It's probably a smart idea that I do the same. When I get back to the car, he is there, waiting for me.

"Should we eat lunch?" I ask.

"Sure. I'm not really hungry, though. Big breakfast."

I laugh, remembering our faces when his plate came out.

"We could always buy sandwiches now and eat them later."

We walk over to the deli to see what they offer. Ryan, again, refuses to let me pay. I don't mind, I won't have a source of income when I get to Florida. Just thinking about it makes me nervous. It's hard not to second-guess my choices. I'm leaving so much behind: a good job that I loved and Jon. I don't know what to think about Jon. When it comes to him, I just feel unsettled. It had been my goal for so long to make our relationship work. It feels like I've given up, but had he given up first?

When we get back to the car with our sandwiches, I take over driving. It feels good to have something to do, and Ryan makes a good navigator. I feel somewhat guilty for sleeping instead of helping when he drove.

"If you're tired, feel free to take a nap."

"I'm not tired."

"Well, if you get tired."

"Alright. Hey, Texas! We haven't seen that one yet, have we?" Ryan searches for it on our list.

I'm still winning, but it makes me smile that Ryan hasn't given up yet. While we drive, I ask him about New Zealand. It seems like another world. It's weird thinking it's summer there Ryan tells me The Lord of the Rings movies were filmed there, and fans still visit to see locations from the films. He grew up playing soccer, or football as they called it, and rugby. He was the bane of existence to his older sisters, always messing up their plans. He tells me the funniest story about one of his older sisters having a big party, and he was home and allowed to attend. Well, all of her friends thought it would be hysterical to get him drunk, He had been maybe eleven at the time.

He drank everything they gave him, including at one point, something red. It may have been a daiquiri, but it did not agree with him, and he got sick. He had never been sick like that before, and his vomit was red. He was still so drunk he thought he was throwing up blood. He wasn't but it did not stop him from going to each and every member of the party to say goodbye. You see, he was saying goodbye because he was certain that he was dying.

"I actually remember feeling quite calm about dying. God, I was such a prat. I felt like a right idiot the next morning when I figured out I was still alive. Many of her friends had spent the night. I avoided them all, I was so embarrassed. She is still mates with some of those kids. My sister and her mates still take the piss, sorry still tease me about it."

"I wish I had brothers or sisters."

"I didn't growing up. They were such a pain, and God, when they were teenagers I thought they were mad. Now that I'm older, I get how lucky I was to have them. They used to beat the crap out of me, and I deserved it but they were my fiercest protectors if anyone else said a foul word towards me."

"You're lucky to have that."

"I am. I know it."

Ryan asks me if I have any embarrassing tales from my childhood. I tell him about my dad and what an outdoorsman he was.

"He loved camping and hiking, fishing, really almost anything outdoorsy. He also loved owls. I always tried to please him, and one morning when I was playing in a park near our home, I saw what I thought was an owl. It was really a large hawk, but I was little and couldn't tell the difference. I wasn't sure why but the hawk landed not far from me and looked at me. I became convinced I would be able to get it to follow me home and give it to my father as a gift. Using a, 'here, birdy birdy' I tried unsuccessfully to get it to follow me. A neighbor saw me near the bird and came and shooed it away. He then yelled at me, saying how unsafe it was for me to be near that kind of bird. I was devastated. Not only had I learned it wasn't an owl, but he'd made me feel silly. I remember going home in tears at my failure."

"That's a lovely story, Grace. I can tell how much you cared for your dad."

I nod, keeping my eyes on the road. If I look at him right now I'm pretty sure I'll cry. I feel overwhelmed by sadness in leaving my home. It's where I had grown up. Where my parents had died. I think to *that* day, the day I stood on the banks of the Cuyahoga and watched their ashes sink into the river. It feels like I am abandoning them somehow. I don't speak much after that. We fly through the Carolina's but get snarled up in Georgia. We finally reach an exit on the far side of the city and call it a day. There had been some small hope of reaching Tampa that night, but we're tired and decide to make a fresh start of it the next morning. I don't mind the delay. It only means another day before accepting I do not live in Cleveland anymore. We find a hotel and get checked in, again with two double beds. This place is much nicer and more updated than the motel we had stayed in the night before. I pass the bed closer to the door and set my bag on the one further away.

"Room service?"

"That sounds wonderful. I don't want to get back in the car anytime soon," I reply.

"My treat."

I smile at him and shake my head. He had tried to pay for the room this time, but I refused. It didn't feel right. He already paid for his plane ticket and didn't let me pay him back. I won't let him pay for either of the rooms. We take our time looking at the menu. I end up ordering pancakes, which makes Ryan laugh. I like breakfast foods, and the only other thing that sounds appealing to me is a hamburger, and we've already had that two nights in a row. Ryan orders a chicken dish and dessert for both of us.

I don't feel the same sense of overwhelming exhaustion I felt the day before. Today, home feels so far away. I still wonder if I live somewhere else, will it still be my home? I had not realized how hard this would be. I thought I wasn't leaving anything behind. Now I understood better how that had been wrong. I'm confused about Ryan. I wonder if he likes me. I guess I know he likes me, but wonder if he likes me likes me. There had been that night at Kate's when I thought he might kiss me. Do I even want him to like me like that?

He's nice, and I'm attracted to him, but I'm just so unsure about everything. Most of all, I'm sad and am not even sure why. It's like there are so many things in my mind that it's overflowing: leaving, missing my parents, feeling like I failed with Jon, being unemployed, not knowing what I have gotten myself into. Each concern washes over me in a seemingly endless loop, some of them lasting longer than others. I wish I had someone to talk to about it. It's a lot to deal with all by myself. The idea of talking to Ryan about it is embarrassing, but I don't know what else to do.

He seems to pick up on it, and while we wait for our food, say, "Grace, you seem a bit down. Everything okay?"

I sit on the edge of my bed "I don't know what's wrong with me. I just feel overwhelmed."

He pulls a chair over and sits in front of me "I can understand how leaving home feels."

"Do you ever get homesick?" I ask, looking down at my hands.

"Sure."

"But you still have family there and a reason to go back" I argue.

He reaches out and puts his hand on mine "Grace, you never need a reason to go back. If you're ever homesick, you can go back and visit any time."

I look up at him "I'm just scared it wouldn't feel like home anymore."

"After some time it probably won't. Things will change, and if you aren't there to see it happen, it will feel strange and different. The first time I went home was after a new shopping center had gone up. I wasn't ready for how different it seemed."

"What did you do?"

"Try and stay busy in the beginning. Too much free time lets you over think things."

"I don't even have a job yet."

He hesitates. "Would you like to work with me?"

"You don't have to do that" I say, shaking my head.

"Seriously."

My mouth drops "But I know nothing about boats or the water."

"I can teach you" he replies, tilting his head to the side.

"I just—I don't know."

"Come on. It'd be fun" he's smiling now.

His hand is still on mine. He moves it when I look down at it "Are you sure?"

"Absolutely."

"You can fire me if I'm awful."

"Grace, don't be silly." he stands and hesitates before pushing the chair back.

I smile, I have a job. I don't give care how much it pays. The idea he would hire me at all…My head turns when I hear the knock at the door. Our food has arrived. I feel a little better. Talking about it had helped. Pancakes too. After we eat, I call Kate let her know we're staying in Georgia for the night because of traffic. Kate is so excited I'm coming she is fine with waiting another day. At this point, we're only five hours away, depending on traffic. We will get there just after lunchtime tomorrow.

Ryan and I stay up talking that night, each in our beds. Ryan doesn't wear a shirt when he goes to bed, just pajama bottoms that hang low on his hips. It feels strange, lying down, turned on my side, talking to him. I have to remind myself not to stare at him. It's hard not to, though. He's turned on his side, head propped up on his hand. He's excited about me coming to work with him. He says we can carpool, and he can teach me everything he knows.

His enthusiasm is infectious, temporarily banishing my gloomy mood. I have to believe I can do this. It's too far to turn back now.

"Grace?"

"Huh?" I squint at him.

"Did you fall asleep?"

"I'm just resting my eyes" I mumble.

"Mm hmm."

"I was." I yawn loudly. "Just a little."

"Alright, Grace. Sweet dreams."

"I'm up. I am," and I'm asleep.

The next morning, I wake up first. I turn to watch Ryan as he sleeps. He's on his stomach with a pillow under one of his arms and head. His hair is in his eyes, and I have the sudden urge to brush it to the side. Recognizing how absolutely creepy that would be, I get up to shower instead. Once I'm dressed I open the bathroom door to let some steam out. I'm brushing my hair when Ryan pops his head in the door, making me jump.

"Didn't mean to startle you. Just wanted to know if the john was free."

"Of course. Here, let me get out of your way."

At the doorway, we both move in the same direction. First left, then right, until I am able to squeeze past him. I feel warm from being so close to him in all of his shirtless glory. I tell myself to slow down when it comes to Ryan. Sure, he flirted with me when I was in Florida. I can still imagine his forehead against my own after our dance. However, since then, he has been nothing but friendly, and now if I'm going to be working with him, it would not be wise to be lusting after him. Most of all, my attraction to him makes me feel guilty. My relationship with Jon, while troubled, has only just ended. What kind of person does it make me to forget those feelings so quickly?

"I'm sorry, what?"

Oh my God, I had been thinking out loud. I clap my hand over my mouth, eyes wide. What had he heard? My reaction seems to confuse him. He cocks his head at me.

I lower my hand. "I hadn't realized I was talking out loud."

"No worries, Grace. I heard you, but I didn't hear what you were saying."

Thank God! "Whew. I was just thinking."

"What were you thinking about?"

"Um, the move" I lie.

His forehead creases. "Okay."

I can tell he doesn't believe me but am grateful that he doesn't press the issue. How embarrassing. Once Ryan is dressed, we head to the lobby together. This hotel has a complimentary breakfast so we won't have to worry about stopping on the way out. It's strange to think I'll be arriving at my new home today. I'm looking forward to seeing Kate and sleeping in that bed again but, I still can't shake off the melancholy.

Ryan drives first, we are maybe five hours from Tampa, and we'll stop halfway for a bite and to refuel. I'll drive the last leg. I want to learn my way around, and Ryan promises to point out important landmarks.

"Do you think you'll apply at any doctors' offices?"

"Probably. It's all I really know how to do."

"Well, you don't have to rush. You can work with me as long as you'd like."

"I don't want to become a pain."

"You?" He seems shocked. "Impossible."

"That is sweet of you to say."

"I am sweet. UTAH!"

I laugh and shake my head at him. Yes, he is very sweet. When it's my turn for the final leg of the trip, the increase of congestion on the road surprises me. What's the big deal on a Monday afternoon? I try to remember if it had been like this when I went with Kate to see the mermaids. One welcome change is the temperature. It must be eighty degrees. I shrug off my green cardigan at a red light.

"Is it always this beautiful?"

"We do get quite a bit of rain, which you have so far missed, but otherwise, yes. It is this beautiful most of the time."

"I might even get a tan."

"That'd be a shame."

I glance at him, one eyebrow raised in a silent question.

He shrugs and looks straight ahead. "You have lovely skin."

I don't say anything. Part of me wants to argue his compliment, to say, 'but my skin is so pasty.' Instead, I allow myself to accept his compliment and maybe even believe it, making a mental note to buy sunscreen. When we are less than an hour away, I start to recognize places from my trip before. Little things, a road sign, a shopping center, a school. Ryan laughs each time I shout, pointing out something I think I've seen before.

When we pull into Kate's driveway, I turn excitedly to Ryan and say, "I live here now."

"That you do. Come on. Let's go find Kate."

When we get to the front door, I pause to let Ryan open it, until he reminds me that this is my house now.

"Oh right," I say, pushing open the door. "Kate," I call out. "We're here."

Kate slowly makes her way from the kitchen to greet us, pulling us both into a hug. She raises her hands to my face, placing one on each cheek and kissing me, then does the same with Ryan. After that, we begin unloading my car. Most of the boxes go straight into my new room. The ones that do not fit go in the spare room with the daybed. When Ryan carries my TV in, I can't decide where to put it. After talking with Kate, we decide to switch it out with the smaller TV in her living room. I don't have a cable jack in my new room so Ryan sets the old living room TV in the room with the daybed.

Kate sits in the corner chair and Ryan on my bed while I unpack my clothes. I'm almost surprised to see how much I have since I haven't done much shopping in the last year. Once I have the dresser filled, I confess I need a break.

"Pool?" Ryan asks.

"That sounds wonderful" I admit.

"I might even get in myself," Kate adds.

Kate and Ryan leave so we can all change. I'm the first one in the pool, Kate not long after. Ryan takes longer than I expect. When he finally walks over, he apologizes for the delay. There was a work call he had to take.

"Everything alright?" Kate moves over on the pool step to give him room to pass.

"Nothing big, just a technical issue with the credit card reader, but it's all sorted now."

"This feels so good." I had grabbed a float and am lying on my stomach. "I might just fall asleep."

"Like last night?"

"What happened last night?" Kate asks, looking at Ryan.

"Grace passed out, mid chat."

"I was tired. Moving is tiring" I try to explain.

"It was a first for me, I have to admit." He mock hangs his head in shame. "I didn't know I was so boring."

"You are not boring." I lift my head to look at him.

"Stop teasing her, Ryan." Kate flicks her hand at him, then turns to slowly get out of the pool.

"Need a hand, Kate?"

"I've got it, dear. Why don’t you get a raft like Grace?"

"Brilliant idea," Ryan says, swimming towards me.

"She didn't mean mine," I say, paddling with my arms away from him. "Go get your own."

He swims right up beside me, hands resting on the raft. "But I like this one."

"Don't you dare!"

He moves as though he is going to flip me but stops. "I wouldn't dream of ruining such a pretty view."

I blush and put my head down. He is such a flirt.

"So when did you want to start work?"

I lift my head. Tomorrow feels too soon. I want to get a bit more settled before I do anything. "Would the day after tomorrow be okay?"

"Why don't you take the rest of the week and start on Monday?"

"That'd be perfect."

Kate had gone to get her knitting from inside the house and was now sitting on her wicker loveseat, working away. I watch as her hands move swiftly with the needles.

"What are you making now, Kate?"

"A little sweater." She proudly holds it up.

"That is so cute."

"I could teach you."

"To make that?"

"We'd probably start with something easy, like a scarf or a baby blanket."

"I'd like that."

"Do you want to learn too, Ryan?"

Ryan had grabbed another float and is jumping on it. Once he is comfortable he says, "Nope, I'm good."

"Not manly enough for you?"

"Too manly, actually. I'm terrified of it," he jokes.

"Silly boy." Kate is shaking her head.

Ryan just grins at us, making us laugh. Not long after, I help Kate get dinner started. We're having salmon and rice with steamed edamame. I'm not sure about knitting but know I want to learn how to cook while living with Kate. Ryan walks in and out a few times, getting plates and silverware to set the table.

"White wine?" Kate asks, winking at me.

"I'll have a beer for myself and open a bottle for the two of you."

"He hates white wine." Kate thinks this is funny for some reason.

We eat on the lanai, and Ryan does not stay long after, wanting to make an early start the next day. I clear the table and load the washer before turning in myself. I have to move some things from the bed to the floor to get in but am asleep in no time. Sometime during the night, I wake up and cannot fall back asleep. My mind is in overdrive, trying to identify unknown sounds of the house and outside my window. A noise may wake me, but the thoughts I cannot quell are what unsettle me. My mind is a loop of destructive thoughts, on an endless replay.

Is this a mistake? Does Jon still love me? Shit! I sit up with a start. I was supposed to call Jon when I got to Florida but forgot. My cell phone is on the charger next to me. Jon had gotten a new phone before I left, but I'm waiting to change mine, still not sure if I want to keep my old number or get a new Florida number. I punch out a quick text to him, hopeful his ringer is off and that it won't wake him. ***-Made it to Florida, am at my grandmother's. Sorry for the late text. Hope you are doing well.*** I flop back onto my pillows, feeling guilty for sending that text so late. Part of me hopes his ringer isn't off and that he will text me back.

What is wrong with me, I wonder. It is pointless to be concerned with Jon now that I am so far away. Does he really miss me? Will he want me to come back? I think back to the first time I ever saw him, that night at the bowling alley. It had seemed almost magical at the time and is still so vivid in my memory. Everything about him, all of our firsts held prime reality in my conscious thoughts. I missed him, I missed home and my parents. I turned on my side, cradling my phone, still hopeful for a return text from Jon. I pull my knees up to my chest feeling more overwhelmed with each passing moment.

My mind will not rest. I am so focused on all of the wonderful moments with Jon and this overpowering sense of loss. I picture everything that won't happen now because I've left. No wedding, no first home, no family of my own. Tears flow freely as I imagine myself and Jon holding the baby we will never have. Sleep is no longer an option as I watch a light from behind the curtain grow brighter to announce the arrival of the sun. I slowly make my way to the bathroom to wash my face.

Back in my room, I check my phone one last time before going in search of food. No response. Kate is by the pool eating breakfast. I pour myself a cup of coffee and make some toast before joining her. She asks how I slept. I know the dark circles under my eyes probably answer the question for her, but downplay it and say I slept fine. I can tell she isn't buying it but am relieved that she doesn't push the subject. We discuss our plans for the day. Kate is to play tour guide as I get my car registered.

I plan to call my insurance company first to file the change of address. I make that call not long after breakfast but before I shower. My insurance is almost doubling. That job Ryan offered me is looking more like a life preserver now. I shower and dress simply in loose capri cargo-style pants and a long-sleeved, striped t-shirt. Kate is in the kitchen pulling out some meat from the freezer to thaw.

"All set, Grace?"

"Yes. I mean, if now is a good time."

"Of course. Let's go."

After my car is registered and its emissions tested, we make our way back to Kate's house. On the way back, Kate asks me what I think of Ryan.

"What do you mean?"

"Do you fancy him?"

"I'm not sure what you mean. I like him. He's a really nice guy."

"Would you ever like to be more than friends with him?"

"Kate, are you trying to set me up?"

"So what if I am? Ryan is such a sweet boy. You could do worse."

"I'm just not sure if I'm ready for anything like that. Besides, it would be weird working for him." I feel like I'm getting ahead of myself. "And most important, who knows if he likes me?"

"I think he does" she says with a sly grin.

"Well, has he said anything?"

"Not directly, no—" I frown.

"Well, there you go. No point in even thinking about it."

"But he's so handsome."

"Then you date him" I tease.

She laughs. "If I was fifty years younger, I would. Hell, if I was thirty years younger, I'd at least think about it."

I laugh and shake my head. As attractive and sweet as Ryan is, there is no way of knowing if he is interested, and most importantly, if I can even handle it. The smartest thing I can do for myself is to get settled before I even think about anything like that. No point in worrying about Ryan when I'm losing sleep over Jon. I check my phone again when we get back to Kate's. No message. Pleading exhaustion, I take a nap. When I wake up, Kate is by the pool knitting. I missed lunch.

When Kate sees me, she says, "There's a plate for you in the microwave."

I'm already enjoying living with such a good cook. I reheat my lunch and bring it out to eat. Kate's knitting group is meeting the next day so she's working on finishing another prayer shawl.

Kate senses my interest in what she is doing. "Would you like to learn?"

"Sure, if it wouldn't be any trouble."

She sets her work on her lap and reaches into the basket beside her for a skein of pale yellow yarn and two thick metal needles.

"Why are these needles so much bigger than the ones you are using right now?" I ask when she hands them to me.

"I think it's easy to learn on bigger needles and the work will go faster as well. It's nice when you are first starting out to see progress."

Kate pulls maybe half an arm length of yarn loose from the skein and shows me how to make the first knot on the needle with the excess yarn hanging down. She then loops the excess yarn with the yarn from the skein to create more loops on the needle. "This is called casting. Every knitting project starts like this. It just depends on what you are making as to how many stitches you need. This scarf will need less than the shawl I'm making."

Kate hands the one needle with the loops to me. "Try adding a couple more stitches."

I add three, and Kate seems pleased. She takes the needle back and shows me how to put the point of the other needle into the loop closest to the narrow end of the needle. Once both points are in, that first loop Kate pulls from the skein to add another loop, pulling it through the first loop. I watch her work that first row. The stitches move from the first needle to the second needle with each new loop.

"When you finish each row, you just turn the needle and start over." Kate passes the needles to me and watches as I slowly make new stitches. When Kate knits, she barely looks at her hands. Me, I have to concentrate on making each new loop.

"Why are they getting so small? It's hard to even put my needle in the loop," I ask.

Kate leans over to look at my needles "Oh, you're working too close to the point. Make sure to put the needle further through to keep it from getting so snug. If you only work the point of the needle, the loops will be too small to push further onto the needle." To illustrate this, Kate holds up her shawl and slowly knits a couple of stitches.

I watch and try to duplicate Kate's movements, although not at her speed. I work to make my loops further down the needle and continue row by row. When I'm ten rows up, I count my stitches and see I now have twenty-seven, not twenty-five. When I show Kate, my mouth drops as Kate begins unraveling all of the work I have just done. I had added two stitches somewhere along the way, and Kate tells me to count each stitch to ensure I won't do it again. But all that work? I take my scarf back and now count each stitch. I am concentrating so intently I don't hear Ryan walk in.

"And what are you making, Grace?"

I jump.

"I didn't mean to startle you. You scare easy, or I'm truly a ninja"

I laugh "I'm sorry. A ninja? Really? I just—never mind. I'm making a scarf," I say proudly, holding up my knitting.

Ryan touches the ribbing delicately. "It's lovely, Grace."

I flush. "I have an excellent teacher."

"Yeah, Kate's brilliant. Did you know she made me a sweater?"

"I did not." I turn to look at Kate.

Now it's Kate's turn to blush. "It was nothing."

"I'll hear none of that. It's my favorite one."

I look down and smile, adding row after row to my scarf. I have little to add to Kate and Ryan's conversation. It's hard to talk to someone while looking down the whole time and counting in my head. They don't seem to mind. Hopefully Kate can tell I'm enjoying my work. I eventually set it aside to help her with dinner while Ryan sets the small table by the pool. This time, I'm a more active participant during our meal.

"How was work?"

"Good. Not very busy," he gestures to the sky. It's somewhat overcast.

The sky is dark gray with heavy clouds that threaten rain. "Did it rain?"

"Not here. Closer to work, yes."

My first day without sun in Florida. It certainly fits my mood. I clear the table then go back to my scarf. There is something in the repetitive needle, loop, pull, count that soothes me. Kate and Ryan stay at the table, chatting over wine and occasionally looking over at me. Before long, the scarf is the length of my arm. I stop and proudly hold it up to show them. Kate comes over to sit by me to inspect it. I hold my breath, fearing she will unravel it again. Instead, she calls me a natural and hands it back to me.

Ryan excuses himself not long after, and we go inside. I stay up, working on my scarf. There is something thrilling in taking loose string and making something tangible with it. I can wear this, maybe not often in Florida, but still. I am making something I can actually wear. After getting up to go to the bathroom, I'm surprised to see how late it is. Setting my project aside, I go to sleep. I had not known how tiring knitting could be. That, with the late hour, gives me little trouble sleeping.

The scent of coffee wakes me the next morning. I look out the window. It's still gloomy, but I can see a hint of sun trying to break through. I wash up before heading into the kitchen. After pouring myself a cup of coffee, I join Kate by the pool. Kate had made a plate of fruit and cheese with a loaf of pear bread on the side. There is plenty for the both of us. I thank Kate when she hands me a smaller plate.

"Did you stay up knitting?"

"I did. My scarf is almost twice as long now. I meant to ask you yesterday. How will I know when to stop?"

"If I make a scarf for myself, I try to make it long enough to loop around my neck a couple times. You can test it out using what you have so far."

"Thanks. I will."

"Grace, would you like to come with me to my knitting group today?"

"Sure! Is that okay?"

"Why wouldn't it be?"

"I don't go to church."

"That's fine. You don't have to go to church, but if you ever want to, just let me know."

"Alright. I'd love to go with you today."

"Great." Kate gets up quickly, and I look at her in confusion. "I'm just going to call my friend to let her know I don't need a ride."

I nod and finish my breakfast. After taking a shower and getting dressed, I pick up my knitting and sit in the living room while Kate gets ready. I try to wrap my knitting around my neck and can get it to go around almost twice but very tightly and with no excess. I get back to work, still counting each stitch. There is one row where I almost add an extra stitch, but I catch myself as I do and stop. The existing stitches that I'm knitting into sometimes fray and look like more than one stitch. That's what I have to watch for.

When Kate comes out, she seems surprised by how far I am on my scarf. "Did you stay up all night?"

"Not all night," I confess.

We take my car, and Kate directs me to her church. It's a large, white Spanish-style Catholic church.

"This is beautiful," I say as we walk in, taking in the stained glass windows.

"Thank you. Those windows are newer. We had to have them replaced after a hurricane five years ago."

We enter through a side door and go down a hallway past some bathrooms to a small room with a table and chairs. There are already a few women there either sitting, already knitting, or gathered by a second smaller table that has some cookies and coffee set out. Kate introduces everyone who is there to me. I'm surprised by how excited they all are to meet me. It's clear she has been speaking of me frequently during their weekly meetings. She directs me to one end of the table and gets settled while I snag a plate with some cookies. As more ladies flow in, they all come over to Kate to meet me. It's cool to see how proud she is to show me off to all of her friends.

Kate had finished her shawl last night, and it goes with maybe five other completed projects to be used for the parishioners. The group makes mostly shawls for people in their church who are either struggling with an illness themselves or of a family member and for family members who may have recently lost someone. Once a month, their priest will come and pray over the completed shawls. They're supposed to represent an embrace of God's love. I wasn't raised in any structured religion but feel I could have been comforted in having something like that after losing my parents so suddenly.

Making my scarf is fun, but the idea of giving someone comfort during a difficult time is speaking to me, it feels like something I have to do. I want to make one as soon as I can. I'm not able to do much knitting during the meeting. All of the ladies want to hear about me and the move. I do my best to answer their questions, even when they start asking me about my nonexistent love life. My thoughts drift to this morning where I had again checked my phone for a message from Jon. Part of me thinks I'll never get one and that I should move on. It's just easier for me to hold out hope.

I have to laugh when they start asking me about Ryan. He appears to have a following amongst the knitting ladies. I bite back a smile as Kate explains he had given her a ride here a couple of times, and one time, walked her in carrying something. He made something of an impact on the ladies who were there. They want to know anything I know about him and just about swoon when I tell them he offered me a job on our drive from Cleveland. At this point, Kate adds that he took me out dancing when I was here the last time, making me blush.

The meeting is over before long, and I say goodbye to all of my grandmother's friends. I make grilled cheese sandwiches when we get back to the house. After lunch, Kate lays down while I work on my scarf. I stop when I get close to the end of the skein, not sure what to do and wondering if Kate has any more yellow yarn because the scarf still isn’t long enough. I log onto my laptop and begin a job search for medical receptionists. It's great that Ryan will hire me in the mean time, but that doesn't seem like something I'll be able to do forever.

There are plenty of doctor's offices, but few are hiring. I email my resume and the referral letter to a couple of places and then log off. Walking over to the window, I see the sun has made its appearance and decide to go for a swim. I had little use for my one suit in Cleveland. Now that I live in Florida, I may need to invest in a few more. I'm still in the pool when Ryan comes over. He takes off his shirt and joins me. I tease him about all the ladies from the knitting group. He loves it. Kate comes out not long after and starts knitting.

Kate has a lasagna in the oven for dinner that night. While she knits, I ask her if she has any more yellow yarn, and if she does, how to connect it to the yarn I'm already working with. I get out of the water to go inside and get my scarf. I sit next to Kate as she walks me through it. Leaving a bit of excess, she just makes the next loop with the new yarn and continues to the end of the row.

"But what do we do now with the pieces hanging out?"

"If you weave them through going back a little, you will never see them." Kate pulls one of the strings back and forth through the row that has just been completed until I cannot see it anymore. "Now, when you are using smaller needles, you probably need to do that with a crochet hook and not your fingers."

When she passes the needles back to me I grin, eager to knit some more.

"Kate, you've created a monster."

I look up like WHAT? Kate just laughs and pats me on the shoulder. I'm still damp, so I move to sit in a plastic armchair instead of the loveseat. I finish a few more rows and then go back inside to cook some broccoli to go with our meal after changing out of my suit. After we finish eating, Ryan asks what I have planned for my last few days of freedom.

"I need to buy some new bathing suits."

"I'll help," Ryan replies eagerly.

I make a face at him and then continue. "I was figuring I would probably need to wear one at work, right?"

"You'll probably start mainly working in the office, and then we'll go from there so you don't have to get anything right away if you don't need it otherwise."

"I won't be in the water right away?"

Ryan sees that I look upset by this. "Do you want to be? I just figured I'd ease you into it, but if you want to, well, what I'm trying to say is, it's up to you."

"But you're the boss. It's up to you."

"Right. Well, I don't feel like your boss, Grace." He sounds putout.

I gulp "What do you feel like?"

"Uh, your friend. So if you want to be in the water I'll put you in the water."

"I want to be in the water." I smile, shyly.

He doesn't hesitate. "Done"

I grin and go back to knitting. Since I've learned what I'm doing when I accidentally add stitches, I pay extra attention to the loops and only count every tenth row or so. This improves my ability to follow the conversation and enables me to actually participate in it. I still move slowly in comparison to Kate and I have to watch what I'm doing whereas she rarely looks down. But I feel an intense feeling of satisfaction when I ask Kate how to end the scarf.

"It's called binding off, dear. Now take your needle and go through two stitches instead of one and then make your loop like normal. Alright, now push the new loop back onto the needle with all of the other stitches. Okay, and then put your needle through the first two loops again.

See? You just do that all the way to the end and pull the lose yarn through."

It feels awkward, but I slowly bind off all of the open loops. With the exception of needing to trim the loose yarn at the end, it is done. I swing it around my neck a few times and model it for them before running inside to see how it looks in the mirror in my room. I tilt my head as I gaze at my reflection. I love it. Sure, I'll probably have little use for a scarf in Florida, but the fact that I had made it myself is enough for me. Next, I decide I want to make a shawl for Kate.

When I come back out, Ryan stops me in the kitchen. He's making bowls of ice cream for Kate and himself and asks if I want one as well. Not one to turn down ice cream, I hang out with him while he makes mine, asking for extra whipped cream. He raises a brow at me, which somehow makes me feel warm and silly for asking. I grab my bowl and Kate's before hurrying outside. I fumble Kate's bowl as I set it on the table beside her, blushing since Ryan is right behind me and sees it. I try to avoid his eyes as I sit down but can sense his gaze on me. I glance up at him just as he's putting a spoonful of ice cream in his mouth. His eyes hold mine in an almost sensual way. I feel my breath catch as he slowly drags the spoon from his lips.

My eyes snap back down to my bowl before I close them. Then I hear him chuckle. That man. Turning to focus my attention on Kate, I ignore him, hoping he will get the hint. How am I going to work with him? Deciding that whatever he may or may not be doing is most likely all in my head, I feel calmer. When I finish my dish, I collect all of them and take them to the kitchen. When I come back out, I see Ryan has left without even saying goodbye. I brush aside how that makes me feel because it seems silly, like an overreaction.

Twisting my hair up into a knot, I watch Kate knit. "Kate, could you teach me how to make a prayer shawl?"

"Of course. You could just make one like your scarf. The only difference is adding more stitches at the start."

"But the way my scarf came out looks different than yours."

"I'm purling every other row."

"Is that different than knitting?"

"Here, let me finish this row, and I'll show you."

I move over to sit by Kate as she completes her row. Kate explains that with knitting I take the point of my needle and put it upwards into the first loop. To purl the stitch, Kate instead positions her needle to enter the stitch pointing downward. She even passes her knitting to me so I can try a couple stitches. It seems easy enough and makes the stitches on one side of the shawl look smaller and closer together, whereas how I knit before, the stitches look almost ribbed. Kate pulls her basket of supplies and lets me pick out some yarn. I choose a multi-colored skein shaded in various saturations of taupe.

On my scarf, Kate had me cast on twenty-five loops. For the shawl, I need sixty. Kate tells me to knit the first five rows just as I had with my scarf, that it will create a nice border. I get right to work. It's different having so many stitches on my needle. I still count each of those first five rows, not wanting to add or drop any and have Kate unravel it. When I finish my fifth row, Kate again works me through how to purl. It feels awkward. I'd become accustomed to holding my hand one way, but now I have to hold my right hand a breath higher and point down instead of up.

I drop a couple of stitches and need Kate's help to fix it. We sit in comfortable silence as we knit. I'm concentrating so intently on the shawl that when Kate tells me she is going inside to bed it startles me. I decide to do the same once I finish the row I'm working on. Kate mumbles something about having created a monster and walks back inside. I smile to myself, and once my row is done, go inside, locking up behind me. I don't knit anymore that evening. Instead, I power up my laptop and check my email to see if I received a response from either of the offices I sent my resume to.

I haven't. Not wanting to shut my laptop so soon, I start surfing the Internet. I don't have a purpose in mind, randomly going over to Pinterest and pinning or liking things I think are cute or funny. Almost distractedly, I create a board for knitwear, thinking I'll ask Kate to teach me to make some of these things. I'm looking at pictures of knit hats when the photo of a boy in a kayak catches my eye. The water in the picture is smooth, like silk. Maybe he's on a lake. The angle of the photo is of his back. He wears a long-sleeved, green t-shirt under an orange life vest. He has longish hair that just peeks out from the bottom of the knit cap he wears.

I pin the picture, not for the hat but because it reminds me of the day I went kayaking with Ryan. I can still picture the way his arms looked as he paddled in front of me. Curious, I open a new browser and Google Erickson Gulf Water Sports. When the page comes up, there's a photo of Ryan and someone I assume is Jack on the home page. They both wear polo shirts and visors with the Erickson logo. I click on the picture to enlarge it. They're both very tan, but working outside, that's to be expected. The person I think might be Jack is blonde and wears sunglasses in the picture. Ryan isn't wearing any and is squinting. I think he is adorable.

Jack is handsome. I can imagine the attention he and Ryan would get if they went out together. Ryan looks to be a couple of inches taller than him, but Ryan is very tall. I shake my head. I've no idea if the person in the photo is Jack or not. I bookmark the page before shutting down my computer. Once in bed, I feel conflicted in my attraction to Ryan. First, part of me is still getting over Jon. Second, in three short days, he is going to be my boss. Third, while he had been very flirty with me the last time I had been here he currently seems less interested.

The next morning, I am up and in the kitchen before Kate. I start the coffee and unload the dishwasher while I wait for it to brew. Kate comes out not long after. We eat bagels with cream cheese by the pool. Then she asks what my plans for the day are.

"I'm going to go buy a few new swim suits today. Would you like to come?"

"No, thank you, dear. But I did make a hair appointment if you could drop me off on your way."

"Of course. What are you having done?"

"Just a trim. My hairdresser is an old friend. We mainly gossip."

"Maybe I could get her to trim my hair, get rid of my split ends."

"I can call Michelle and see if she can fit you in today."

"That would be great."

Kate's hairdresser is able to squeeze me in before Kate. After my cut, I go to the mall and plan to pick Kate up on my way back. Michelle is a hoot. She's a tall, leggy blonde with a salon out of her house. She gives me a razor trim, and I love the way it turns out. She recommends a hair serum I can use while I work out on the gulf to help minimize future damage. I play with my hair as I drive to the mall, loving how light and soft it feels. I have to check the directory to find the suit shop. I don't stay there long. All of the suits are too skimpy or fancy to work in.

I find another directory, and this time go to a sports store. I buy three one-piece suits and a couple of sports bra styled, two-piece suits. When I get back to Michelle's, Kate's hair is almost done. Both Kate and Michelle want to see my new suits, so I run back to my car to grab the bag. Holding each one up as they ohhh and ahhh over them.

"You should have picked something a little sexier if you're going to be working with Ryan," Michelle teases.

Another fan, I think to myself. When Kate's hair is done, we drive back to her house. For lunch, we have a chef salad. Kate lies down afterward, and I do a small load of laundry to wash my new suits. While the wash is going, I work on my shawl. I can't wait to give it to Kate. She's become such a huge part of my life, and I want to give her something to show her how much this means to me. Maybe she can use it to comfort herself, given all the loss she dealt with over the years. Each time I walk down the hallway to my new room, I still pause to look at the family photo. I have no children but cannot imagine how Kate felt losing both of hers.

Acceptance

the act of accepting
-Merriam Webster

Over that weekend, I try out my new suits. I'm nervous about working with Ryan. On Monday, I wake up early to get ready. Kate fusses over me at breakfast as though I'm a kindergartener getting onto the bus for the first time. She even packs me a lunch and checks to see if I remembered sunscreen. It's nice, motherly. Something I have not felt in over two years.

Ryan pops his head in the front door. "Cinderella's chariot awaits!"

"Well, have her home before she turns into a pumpkin," Kate returns.

I grab my bag and travel coffee mug, double checking to make sure I have my sunglasses and hurry over to him.

"Is what I'm wearing okay?"

Ryan inspects me, starting with my gray cloth sneakers, raising his gaze to my black running shorts and company t-shirt he had dropped off over the weekend. He brings his eyes up to mine. "You'll do."

I smirk at him and roll my eyes.

"Hey, big scary boss man here. No eye rolling missy."

I bite my lips to keep from laughing and solemnly nod, my eyes dancing. I follow him out to his Jeep, turning to wave once more to Kate. As he drives, I sip my coffee, wondering what the day will bring. When we get to the business, Ryan has me hang out with him in the office area. There are small groups that have reservations to use jet skis to help. Ryan and I check them in and take their payments up front. Then every adult and adult guardian has to sign a waiver. Ryan shows me where to file the paperwork for each group. He also shows me how to schedule folks who call in to make reservations.

What strikes me as being funny is how similar it is to working the front desk at the doctor's office. I check people in, have them fill out paperwork, and accept payments. Ryan is impressed by how quickly I pick it up. Seeing that the office will not be a big deal for me, he asks if I want to go listen to one of the jet ski briefings. There's a lull in reservations, so once the next group is checked in, I walk with him down to the dock to listen to the safety points. Darrell, one of his other employees, is giving the briefing straight off of the dock, there is a large rectangle marked off with buoys. It's about the size of a football field. Darrell explains how that's the riding zone and how to keep the jet ski in idle when going to and from the dock.

He talks about the automatic kill key that is attached to a bracelet each rider will wear. If someone falls off the key being pulled will turn off the jet ski. Every rider needs to wear a life jacket, and he goes around to check that they're all on tightly. The dock has steps that lead down into the water. Darrell slowly walks down them, the first rider following him. Once he's set on the ski and headed to the ride zone, he gets the next rider set until they're all out.

He waves at Ryan, and climbing out of the water, walks over to meet me.

"Would you like to go out on one?" Ryan turns, asking me.

"Right now?" I gasp.

"Sure. Hey, Darrell. Tell Jennifer to watch the office. I'm going to take Grace out."

"Will do. It was nice meeting you, Grace."

Ryan pulls off his shirt and sets it on a bench that is built into the dock. When he sees I'm still standing there, he asks. "You're wearing a suit, right?"

"Oh, yes I am" I say, sitting down to take off my shoes, then shirt and shorts.

Ryan grabs a pair of life jackets.

"Would you like to ride with me?"

"Like behind you?"

His face breaks out in a giant grin. "Yeah."

My brows pull together. "You won't go too fast will you?"

"You'll be safe with me."

I gulp, feeling warm all over and watch him. He walks down the steps and over to a ski, tugging it back over to the dock. Once he's on, he holds out his hand to help me get on. I ease myself into position, deliberately moving my hands to the back of my seat. When Ryan turns it to idle, it bounces, causing me to jump and wrap my arms around his waist. There is still some space between us, so Ryan tugs on my legs to eliminate it. The life jacket stops just short of his waist so my arms are on his bare skin. I feel dizzy, sure that it's being this close to Ryan that's making my heart pound. As he makes his way over to the ride zone, I lean against him, my cheek on his shoulder blade.

"Hold tight," is all the warning he gives me once we enter the ride zone.

He isn't going as fast as some of the other riders but fast enough that if he takes a sharp turn, I'd probably fall off. I tense my legs, pressing them tightly to Ryan's. He drops one hand down to my thigh and rests it there. He may mean the gesture to be calming, but it has the opposite effect. His hand seems to burn, and I'm certain he can hear my heart thumping wildly. When he moves his hand to steer, I feel the loss of its presence on my leg. He turns back to look at me in that moment. He sees how sad I look and stops the ski in the middle of the ride zone with skis still going wildly about us.

"Are you okay? Was I going too fast?"

The jet ski bounces up and down in the surf created by multiple wakes. "I'm fine." I turn my face away from his eyes. "You don't need to stop. I like it"

"Are you sure?"

I tighten my arms around him, pressing my cheek to his shoulder blade again and nod. After a beat, we're off again. It's thrilling, soaring over the water as I cling to him, feeling the heat of his skin against my cheek. I wonder if he ever takes anyone else out. The idea of another girl with him…I don't even want to think about it. Ryan stops the ski and asks if I want to try driving it.

"Sure."

He turns, snakes his arm around my waist, and pulls me into his lap. I gasp, putting my hand on his thigh to steady myself. I am settled between his legs, my hand still on his thigh. My back is pressed up against his chest. His hands have not moved from my waist, and his face hovers over my shoulder. My face is turned towards him. If I move an inch I can kiss his cheek. If he turns to look at me, we will almost be nose to nose. He moves his hands to circle my waist as he removes the kill key from his wrist. He takes one of my hands, placed the kill key on it, and lifts my hand to the throttle to clip it back in.

He lifts my other hand from his leg and places both of them on the grips. My back arches as he leans over me, his hands still on mine. I close my eyes and try to catch my breath. It's so hard to concentrate on what he is saying when he seems to be everywhere. The ski rocks us as he shows me how to start it and give it gas. He slowly has me turn the throttle, and I feel the engine jump to life beneath me. Ryan shows me how to steer then wraps his arms around my waist, resting his chin on my shoulder. I go much slower than he had and make a wide loop inside the ride area. After that, Ryan has me switch it to idle and we head back to the dock.

"Your hair smells heavenly," he whispers into my ear.

I shiver, making the jet ski jerk, and he chuckles behind me, running the tip of his nose up and down my earlobe. He sits back when we get closer to the dock. He jumps off first and then helps me, his hands resting on my waist a beat before taking my hand and leading me up the stairs.

"Did you like it?"

I grin. "I loved it."

We are off the stairs and he still has my hand in his. I see Darrell walking over to us. I tug my hand free. Ryan gives me a strange look and takes off his life jacket. I try to do the same but can't seem to get the last clip undone. Ryan pushes my hands away and undoes it for me.

"Was that your first time?" Darrell asks when he reaches us.

I flush and nod.

"So, did Ryan show you a good time?"

What was it with this guy and innuendo? Ryan just laughs and pulls on his t-shirt before handing me a towel. I dry off best I can and put my clothes back on. We walk back to the office together.

"Would you like to have lunch with me today?" Ryan asks as we walk back.

Yes. No. I wasn't sure. "I brought a lunch with me today."

"You could always eat it tomorrow," he pleads.

"Alright."

"Did you want to go to that burger place?"

"You should have said that from the start," I tease.

"Ouch." He puts his hand up to his chest as though wounded.

Jennifer has her feet up on the desk and is filing her nails when we walk up. She glances up at us and slowly lowers her feet but keeps filing her nails.

"Jennifer, this is Grace."

"Figured as much."

I shoot Ryan a concerned look. "This is Jennifer in a good mood. We all stay far, far away from her otherwise."

She nods her head in agreement.

"I'd have fired her ages ago, but she is somewhat of a computer whiz, and we wouldn't have a website without her."

"I prefer computer genius," Jennifer says, looking up from her nails.

"Alright, computer genius. I'm taking Grace to lunch. Want me to bring you back some onion rings?"

Her eyes light up, and she nods before realizing she looks too happy. She leans back into her chair and shrugs.

"Come on," Ryan says, taking my hand again and walking to his car.

His hand feels so warm in comparison to mine. I'm both thrilled and terrified by the physical contact. Ryan walks me to the passenger side and opens my door for me.

Why does this feel like a date? Is this a date? I know I like him. I really like him and not just because I dream about running my fingers through his brown hair. He's a good person. I'm amazed he's single. Must be hard to meet people eating dinner with my grandmother every night.

"Grace, I have to tell you something."

He looks so stressed. "Is everything okay?"

"I hope so. Well, here's the thing. I'm attracted to you."

I inhale sharply. I thought he might be, but I never expected him to be so blunt about it.

"And I think you might feel the same way about me. Do you?"

I feel incapable of responding but reach my hand out to set it on top of his. His eyes snap to mine, and it’s like his whole body relaxes.

"I was really nervous about telling you."

My mouth drops. "You were nervous around me?"

"Since the day I picked you up from the airport."

I don't understand. "But why?"

He gives me a half smile. "I think you're lovely, always have. When I heard you had a boyfriend, I was crushed."

I just shake my head. I can't imagine why he would be interested in me.

"So is this a date?'

"Nope. This is just lunch. If you aren’t doing anything Friday night, I'd like to take you on a date but not just that. I'd like to date you period. Is that something you would be interested in? Dating me?"

"I'd really like that."

His smile at my response is perfection. I laugh when he grabs my hand and kisses it. He is too cute. The rest of lunch is uncomfortable, but in a good way. I find myself transfixed by his lips. I don’t hear a word that come out of them but imagine them on me. When I’m not staring at his lips, I watch his hands, thinking back to when he had pulled me in front of him on the ski. Those hands on my waist. It's hard to eat when I am so distracted. On the way out, Ryan picks up the take out order of onion rings for Jennifer.

When we are back at the office, Ryan leaves me with Jennifer for the afternoon. He is leading a kayak tour. I feel light and can't seem to stop smiling or looking at him.

"So you and Ryan?"

"Yes?"

She tilts her head at me. "Bummer."

"Do you like Ryan?"

She laughs. "Nope. I'm gay. Was kinda hoping you were too, blondie."

My mouth drops. Not really sure what the right response to that is so I just shrug, which makes her laugh. That seems to eliminate any tension that may have been there, and we work well together for the rest of the day. Not long before closing time, I watch Ryan return with the kayak tour. I am riveted watching his arms as his paddle slices through the water. Once he is parallel to the dock, he smoothly pulls himself and his yak out before helping other people. I blush when I remember my fall getting out of the kayak.

After everyone is out of their kayaks and the gear is stowed, Ryan comes to collect me. He takes off his shirt, using it to wipe his face in the office. He grabs a spare one and pulls it over his head. I did my best not to drool, still a bit flustered by the idea of him liking me. When we are in the car, he asks how I got on with Jennifer.

"She was great. I think she really liked me."

He groans. "Did she hit on you?"

I pause. "Not really."

"What did she say?" He glances at me, lifting a brow.

I'm laughing at this point. "Just that she was bummed I was with you."

"Can't blame her. I think Darrell was trying to hit on you, too."

"What?"

"May have to keep you with me at all times."

"Hush. Don't be silly."

"I'm really only worried about next time Jack is in town."

"Your partner? Why?"

"I'm scared you'll take one look at him and forget all about me."

"Not going to happen."

He drops me off at Kate's. We both need a shower. He jokingly suggests we save water and take a joint shower. I do my best to look shocked while images of soaping up his chest flash through my mind. Kate is on the lanai, waiting to hear all about my first day. Ryan and I decide we are going to tell Kate about us together. After chatting with Kate for a few minutes, I hurry to take my shower, wanting to look nice when Ryan comes over. I'm getting dressed when I hear my phone buzz.

Quickly pulling my shirt on, I answer it. "Hello?"

"Hey, stranger!"

"Nikita, how are you?"

"Good, just missing you. So, how's Tampa, tell me all about it."

I tell her about the drive, the weather, my learning how to knit, and saving the best for last: Ryan.

"Shut up! That guy who came and helped you move? Oh my God, he is so friggin' hot. How did it happen?"

"He took me jet skiing today. It was so intense. First, I was behind him, then he was behind me. Then he took me out to lunch and told me he was attracted to me and asked me if I would date him."

"Whoa, and that accent. I am super jealous right now."

"He's taking me out Friday, I'm excited but, I wonder...Do you think it's too soon? I mean, since Jon?"

"Do you still have feelings for Jon?"

"I think I will always miss what we had, sometimes I'm sad when I think about it, or angry, when I think about how he acted. I don't know if I'll ever forgive him, it's weird. I'm not in love with him anymore but we were together for so long it's just complicated."

"I get that, you can't just turn off feelings like that, but I don't think you're rushing. Didn't you say you guys have dinner together every night? Don't stress about it, just do what feels right. How's living with your grandmother? Didn't you say she's helping you make a scarf? Kim just bought a gorgeous scarf off Etsy. Text me a picture of the one you made, and I'll show it to everyone. While you're at it, send a picture of Ryan too. "

I'm just hanging up when I hear Ryan walk in. Crap. I wanted to brush my hair and put on some make up. I should have been multitasking while I was on the phone with Nikita but was too distracted talking. I grab my brush and quickly pull it through my still slightly damp hair. When I turn, he's leaning against my doorframe. Something comes over me, and I rush over to hug him.

His arms wrap around me. "Hey."

"Hi."

"You're going to be trouble. I can tell."

I go to pull away, and he holds me tighter. "No, no. I'm smelling your hair."

I tilt my face up to his and smile. He leans down and softly brushes his lips over mine. Our eyes are locked as he pulls back a breath. The look in his eyes makes me wonder if he acted on impulse. It feels like he is trying to gauge my reaction. I want him to know how happy I am that he kissed me. I put my hands around his neck and pull his lips back to mine. This kiss is not delicate. It is not sweet. Ryan pushes me up against the wall. My hands knot in his hair. His hands pull my hips tightly to him. His lips move to my neck as he pulls one of my legs up to his waist.

I try to catch my breath but can't as long as he is touching me, I gently push him back, and my eyes widen when I see the hunger in his. This is going to be interesting. I bite my lip and grab his hand, pulling him towards Kate. I don't trust myself alone with him right now. Kate is sitting on the lanai, knitting. I keep his hand in mine and pull him into the room with me.

When Kate looks up and sees we are holding hands, she mutters, "Took you two long enough," before going back to her knitting.

"Kate!"

"What? You should've heard him talk about you when you went back to Cleveland."

He does his best to not look embarrassed. "What can I say? I was enchanted from the moment I first met you."

"Really?"

"Really." He leans down, brushing his lips against my cheek.

Kate sets her knitting down beside her and stands to hug and kiss both of us. "I say this is a reason to celebrate. Ryan, go open a bottle of wine." Once he is out of the room, she turns to me. "Are you happy, dear?"

I blush and nod, asking her if she thinks it's too fast.

"It only takes a moment, sweetheart, if it's the right person."

Ryan walks back out with three glasses. After handing

one to Kate and to me, he stands next to me with his arm around my waist.

After taking a drink, I jump. "I forgot. Here, can you hold this?" I hand my glass to Ryan. "Nikita asked that I send her a picture of my scarf. I'll go grab it from my room. Will you take the picture?"

Ryan nods, setting both of our glasses down on the table behind him. I hurry back in, handing him my cell phone. I am wrapping the scarf around my neck when the phone buzzes in his hand. He passes it to me, and I check it. It's a text from Jon. ***I miss you***, is all it says. I close my eyes, and let my hand drop to my side.

"Grace, are you alright?"

I open my eyes and meet Ryan's concerned gaze. "It's nothing." I click to the camera feature of my phone and hand it back to him

Ryan snaps a couple of pictures of me and passes my phone back to me. After making sure I look okay in the pictures, I pick my favorite one and text it to Nikita. I turn off the screen and put it in my pocket as I move to stand beside Ryan.

"Thank you." He slides his arm back around my waist, giving me my glass of wine.

Kate goes into the kitchen to take a casserole out of the oven.

"Are you sure you're alright?" Ryan asks, turning to face me.

"I am. It was a text from Jon. I just didn't expect to hear from him again."

"You don't have to tell me."

"I know. I'm just nervous about liking you so soon after things ended with him."

"I don't want to rush you."

"It's not that. I just worry that you'll think less of me."

"Impossible."

I give him a half smile. He's adorable, and the way he's looking at me makes me feel suddenly shy. It's still hard for me to understand that he's interested in me. I lean against him, putting my head down. Ryan sets his wine glass down and slowly rubs his hands up and down my back. I feel myself relax into him, and he leans his cheek on the top of my head.

"Grace, I want you to know I adore you, and the thought that you might return those feelings makes me very happy." I feel his chest lift as he inhales deeply and I look up at him.

"Your hair smells so good." He playfully runs his nose back and forth in my hair, making me laugh.

"Ryan, stop smelling her and set the table."

"Yes, ma'am," He says, grinning. He kisses me on the cheek before dropping his arms and walking to the kitchen.

Over dinner, I'm hypersensitive to Ryan. He seems to be discreetly touching me, avoiding Kate's notice. His knee bumps mine. His hand accidentally brushes my elbow. I can tell what he is doing. Ryan jumps up to help me when I get up to clear the table.

"I really want to kiss you again," he whispers to me as I load dishes into the washer.

I peek out the window over the sink that opens onto the pool deck to check where Kate is. Seeing her busy with her knitting, I turn and quickly give him a peck on the lips. Ryan informs me that is not the kind of kiss he was hoping for before turning me to face him, his hands tight on my hips. My mouth drops into an o shape as he slowly lowers his lips to mine. At first, his kiss is soft and feather light, but his kiss deepens as he pulls me to him. When I sigh, his tongue caresses my bottom lip before brushing over my own. My hands rise to wrap around his neck as I arch my body into his.

"Am I interrupting?" Kate is leaning on the kitchen table.

I turn quickly and reach for the next plate. "I, um, well, no."

"Yep, Kate. You are definitely interrupting," Ryan says, nuzzling his nose into my hair.

"Ryan!"

"What?"

"He's fine, dear. I just wanted to let you kids know that I'm going to bed." Kate winks at us before turning and going to her room.

I stand there, shaking my head. First, I cannot believe my grandmother just winked at me, and second, we've just barely finished dinner. Kate never goes to bed this early. I can feel the heat coming off Ryan. I just don't know what to do or how far he wants to go. Will he be fine with just kissing? I'm not sure I'm ready for anything else.

"Want to go for a swim, Grace?"

"Okay. I have to change first."

"Alright. You go change, and I'll finish up in here."

I change into one of my new two-piece suits and meet him by the pool. He's already in the water. His head is down, like a crocodile, only his green eyes visible. I slowly make my way down the stairs as he swims over to me. He's in front of me as my foot touches the pool floor. He takes my hand, pulling me to the deeper side. When we stop, I sink down and let the water cover me, standing back up once my hair is wet.

"Like Aphrodite rising from the surf."

"Hush."

"Make me." He wraps his arms around me, pulling me in tight.

I place my hands on his arms, feeling the strength in them. I slide them up to his shoulders and then run my fingers in his hair as I tug his face towards mine. His lips are soft as he molds them to mine. I am drunk off of his touch, his hands trailing lazily up and down my back. His fingertips leave a trail of goose bumps in their wake. I shiver against him, making him pull me closer.

"Are you cold, Grace?" he says, moving his lips to my neck.

I shake my head and wrap my arms tightly around his neck. Suddenly, he pulls away, and I look at him, confused.

"Trying not to rush things."

"Oh."

"You have no idea how badly I want you right now."

I feel heat rush to my cheeks.

"I should probably go before I ravish you on the pool deck."

I don't want him to leave but am not ready for what might happen if he stays. I get out of the pool and grab a towel for each of us. Ryan quickly towels off and hangs it on a hook by the pool. He pulls my towel from my hands and wraps it around my shoulders. He pulls me to him and captures my mouth again.

After kissing me soundly, he nips my ear. "See you in the morning."

I watch him walk across the backyard and to his house. He gives me a smile and wave just before he is out of sight. I go inside, locking up behind me. After changing for bed I look at my phone, still unsure of what to do with Jon's text. Should I even reply? What can I say in response to that? I have a new text. From him? I feel silly when I see it's from Nikita instead. She loves the scarf and wants one herself. She specifically requests a purple one. I'm too amped to sleep, and it's still early. I pull out my shawl project, and I work on it as I think about Ryan and how he makes me feel. Stopping once my hands feel like they are going to fall off, I go to sleep.

Ryan and I fall into a comfortable rhythm, spending most of each day together. On Thursday, Ryan takes a group out fishing and asks if I'd like to be his first mate. The only boat I've ever been on is the kayak. The idea of being so far from the shore is exciting. He's taking a group of six out into the gulf for the day. Darrell is also going. Ryan and Jack own two boats for offshore fishing: a swanky luxury mini yacht named Seabreeze and a simple flats fishing boat named Squirt. The group going out that day consists of local lawyers celebrating a merger. Since they'll be taking Seabreeze, Ryan thinks I'll have fun coming along.

A couple of the attorneys attempt to flirt with me until Ryan announces that I'm his girlfriend and not part of the tour. Hearing that title shocks me. I know we're dating, but it overwhelms me that he already considers me his girlfriend. I'm stressing out over it so much that it must become obvious to him. He pulls me aside to explain he used the term to keep the guys from flirting with me and that he isn't trying to rush me. Does that mean he doesn't want me to be his girlfriend? I curse myself for my emotions being so all over the place. I don't know how to feel about him calling me his girlfriend. Now it seems to bother me that he may not have meant it. Our first official date is tomorrow. I still have no idea where he's taking me.

The charter trip is fun but more work than I'd expected. When Ryan drops me off, I tell him I'll probably eat something and go straight to bed. The next day, I stay in the office having had too much sun the day before.

We're busy but somehow the day still seems to drag. I'm counting down the minutes until my date. I'm having fun working with him, even though I spent Friday in the office he makes a point to swing by and steal kisses whenever he's free. I feel so comfortable around him, it doesn't stop my heart from racing each time he is near me.

I absentmindedly check the time on my cell phone. I have a text from Nikita asking me how her scarf is coming along. I finished the shawl for Kate but haven't given it to her yet. I want it to be special, like a gift to thank Kate and make sure she knows how much everything she does means to me. I haven't even started the scarf. I'm not even sure if Kate has purple yarn or if I will need to go buy some. I'm really getting into the idea of creation, of how cool it feels to make something. I even talk to Ryan about it during one of our drives into work. He tells me I'm adorable and if I like I can knit at work whenever we're slow.

"Grace?"

I look up. "Sorry."

"Did you hear what I asked?" Jennifer huffs.

"I didn't. What's up?"

"So do you know where you guys are going tonight?"

"Ugh. No, and it's driving me crazy. I don't like surprises, and I'm not sure how to dress. Ryan says anything is fine but that doesn't help."

"Have you guys done it yet?"

"Jennifer!"

"Is that a yes or a no?"

"It's a none of your business."

"Oh, come on. You guys live right next door to each other, and I've totally seen you making out with him when you think no one is watching."

I flush. "Either way…"

"If you haven't, do you think tonight will be the night?"

I hadn't thought about that. What if that's what he's planning? I look down to the dock where Ryan is standing. His back is to me. He must have just gotten out of the water. I can see drips of water coming off of his suit as it clings to him in a mouthwatering way. It's like he can sense my eyes, and he turns to look back at me. He waves, so I blow him a kiss. Instead of playfully catching it like your average male, Ryan sprints to me and kisses me soundly. When he finishes, Ryan takes in my glazed expression with twinkling eyes and is off again back to the dock.

"You guys are so doing it tonight," Jennifer mumbles to herself.

I feel warm all over at the thought. I check the time again and sigh, thinking it's not moving fast enough. The sound of a little black sports car squealing into their parking lot startles me.

"Da na na na." Jennifer hums "Bad to the Bone."

"Someone you know?"

"Yep. Jack's back."

Oh, Jack, the partner with a bad case of wanderlust. I wonder if he even knows who I am or that I'm working here. I stand as he approaches us.

Whether he knows who I am or not is quickly answered with a, "So this must be Ryan's girl."

I redden and put out my hand.

Jack instead pulls me into a hug. "Lucky guy."

"Unhand my woman, scoundrel" Ryan walks up grinning.

"You never were good at sharing." Jack releases me and greets Ryan with a light punch on the shoulder.

"This is a surprise. What brings you into town?"

"My oldest, confirmed bachelor best friend meets a girl he can't stop talking about. I was too intrigued not to come see what all of the fuss was about."

I feel like locking myself in the bathroom, I don't know if I've ever felt this evaluated before. Ryan comes to stand next to me, wrapping his arm around my waist. I shoot him a confused look, and he shrugs, waiting for the evaluation to be complete.

After another moment, Ryan says, "Well?"

"She's smoking. Well done, you. Sure you won't share?"

My mouth drops.

"No chance."

"Worth a shot."

"I'm still standing here" I add.

"Right. Grace, this is Jack. Jack, this is Grace."

"We've met."

"So really, why are you in town?"

"Bored mainly. Think Kate will mind another for dinner?"

"It will just be the two of you. Grace and I have plans tonight."

"I can call her," I offer, pleased my date is still on.

"That'd be great."

I grab my cell and dial Kate. When I explain, a third time that Jack is in town and would like to come for dinner, my grandmother sounds thrilled.

"Well, that's settled. So, where are you two headed tonight?"

"That's a surprise."

Jack turns to me. "Need a lift home?"

"I already have a ride," I say confused.

"Come on. It'll give you more time to primp, and I can hang out with Kate."

"I don't primp."

"Ever?" He seems shocked.

"Well, I guess sometimes." This really is the strangest conversation.

"And for tonight?"

"I have no idea where we are going." I glance up at Ryan. "He said to wear anything I'd like."

"That sounds clothing optional to me."

Who is this guy?

Ryan looks down at me. "It's not that kind of date."

"Bummer. Those are the best kind." He turns to Jennifer. "Still only into chicks?"

"Fraid so."

"So how long will you be in town?"

"Maybe a week. Can I crash in the spare?"

He hesitates. "Sure. In fact, it's almost quitting time. Jennifer, can you close up?"

She nods, and he turns to lead me out of the office. I stop, turning back to grab my purse and wave goodbye to Jennifer before reaching for his hand. Jack pulls out in front of us and speeds off.

"Well he's interesting."

"Jack's a character."

"And a flirt."

"Definitely a flirt. Good thing I asked you out before he got here."

"Why?"

"The girls go for Jack."

"Not for me. Thanks. My friend Nikita would be all over him, besides you have the hot accent."

Ryan relaxes "Hot? Well, when you put it that way."

Jack is parked in front of Kate's house when we pull up.

"So what time are you picking me up?"

"Seven. Feel free to primp."

"Good to know," I say, leaning over to give him a kiss.

He puts his hand on the back of my neck and deepens it. When I pull back, he has a dreamy expression on his face. He looks so cute I give him another quick peck before getting out of the car. I can hear Kate and Jack out by the pool. His voice carries, and I laugh when I realize he's flirting with Kate. I can tell Kate's loving every second of it.

"Hello, Kate. Jack."

"Oh, Grace, dear. Come sit with us. Jack was just telling me the funniest story about this girl in Brazil."

"Can't. I've been told to 'primp.'" Then I remember Nikita's text. "Kate, do you have any purple yarn?"

"Another knitter?" Jack asks.

"I taught her myself. And yes, dear, I do." Kate beams and then reaches into her basket for a couple skeins.

Taking them, I thank her before heading to my room. Once there, I regard my closet. Primp. That means dressed up, right? But how dressed up? I settle on a black maxi skirt with a white V-necked tank and pair it with a wide brown leather belt and sandals. I take a quick shower and shave my legs. After changing into my outfit, I dry my hair and put on some make up. Not much, mainly my eyes and some lip gloss. I think about curling my hair, but it seems like a wasted effort. Without tons of hairspray, the curls will never hold. I wear it down but slip an elastic around my wrist in case I want to pull it up.

After a spray of perfume, I grab one skein and my needles and sit with Kate and Jack.

"I must be losing my touch," Jack says, shaking his head a few minutes later, looking at the two of us knitting.

I have to laugh. That's pretty funny.

"So what are you making, Grace?"

"A scarf for one of my friends in Cleveland."

"How long does it take to make one?"

"Not long. Maybe three days if I knit in the evenings."

"You could sell them."

"No one would ever buy something from me."

"You'd be surprised. There's this website I heard about called something like Easy…Tesey."

"Etsy?"

"That's it. I was talking to someone on my plane over about it."

"One of my old co-workers bought a scarf like this from there."

"You should find out how much she paid for it." He turns to Kate. "How much do each one of those balls of yarn cost?"

"These? Maybe three dollars, but there are more expensive options."

"How many balls—"

"Skeins," she corrects.

"How many skeins does it take to make a scarf?"

"If it is really wide or long, at least two."

"That's all? You could make a serious profit."

"Talking numbers again?" Ryan pops his head around the corner.

Seeing how he's dressed, I'm happy with my outfit. He's wearing a pair of tan khakis and a charcoal grey dress shirt, sleeves rolled to his elbows. He leans down to give Kate a kiss on the check, never taking his eyes off of me.

"Telling Grace she should try and sell her scarves."

"You might want to listen to him, Grace. Jack has very good business sense."

"I'll think about it," I say, standing and walking over to Ryan.

"You look lovely," he breathes into my ear, making me shiver.

"You kids have fun tonight." Kate waves us off.

I wonder if it's so she can be alone with Jack again. Looks like Kate's a flirt too. Ryan holds my hand as he walks me to his car and opens my door for me.

"So do I get to know where we're going yet?"

"Nope. Still a surprise."

I'm not expecting us to go to work. "Um, did you need to pick something up from the office?"

"You'll see."

He comes around and opens my door. I've never been here at night. There are white Christmas-style lights wrapped around the railing of the dock, and the Seabreeze is lit up similarly, with lights coiled around the metal guards. He takes my hand and leads me down to the dock. He helps me onto the boat, and I see there is a table set on its deck.

"This is beautiful, Ryan."

"This is nothing. You are beautiful. Want to drive?"

"But it's dark out."

"So is that a no?"

"How will I know where to go?"

"You'll have me."

Ryan unties the ropes securing the boat to the dock and uses a long wooden pole to push it clear. He has it away from the dock before he motions for me to come and take the wheel. He stands behind me, hands resting on my hips. He whispers directions in my ear. I look back to watch the lights from the shoreline grow smaller. The water is fairly calm. Once we're maybe twenty minutes out, he cuts the engine and drops the anchor. The moon is near full and out over the water. It gives more light than I'd have expected. It's as though its glow is diminished by all of the electric lights I'm accustomed to.

We sit, and I laugh when Ryan pulls out a bag of take out and milkshakes from the burger joint. I figure he must have had help, maybe Jennifer. He even remembers I like artichokes on my burger. As we eat, the water gently laps the sides of the boat. This is only my second time sailing, but I can tell how much it means to Ryan. I munch on an onion ring, belatedly worrying over my breath. Will it matter since he is eating them too? When I excuse myself to use the restroom, I'm thrilled to see a bowl of mints below deck.

Ryan is cleaning up when I come back up. After stowing a trash bag, he crooks his finger at me, motioning me to come to him. He's crouched when I stand in front of him. He slowly rises, running his hands up the sides of my legs as he does. My breath catches in my throat as I think back to what Jennifer had said. Does he want to sleep with me? Tonight? There's a cushioned bench behind him, and he tugs me down with him as he sits. I am in his lap, my legs draped over to one side.

My hands are on his shoulders. He has one arm tightly wrapped around my waist. His other arm starts on the small of my back and slides upward and under my hair to the back of my neck. He pulls my face to his. My arms tighten around his neck when he bites my lip. I moan when he moves his lips to my neck and then lower, to the curves visible from the top of my V-neck. The bench is wide enough for him to shift us to where we are lying side by side. He gently runs his fingers up and down my arm, laughing at the sea of goose bumps his fingers leave in their wake. Shivering, I move closer to him. He moves his hand to my neck. His fingers are in my hair, and his thumb draws lazy circles on my earlobe.

"You are so lovely."

I bury my face in his neck, embarrassed.

"Don't be shy."

I keep my head down, shaking it. This whole thing is so surreal and different from where I was just two months ago. It's hard for me to reconcile that point of my life to now. It almost doesn't feel real. Here I am, on a boat, in the Gulf of Mexico, in the arms of a beautiful man.

"Grace, look at me."

My eyes rise to meet his, and I'm trapped in the intensity of them. We're almost nose to nose, and time seems to stop as I feel his desire. I bite my lip and watch as his eyes drop to my mouth, the corners of his lips turning up as he brings his eyes back to mine. We both turn at the sound of a large splash near the boat.

"What was that?"

"Don't worry. Probably just a big fish." He laughs at my expression. "You're safe with me."

I snuggle back into his arms, and he softly rubs his hand up and down my back. I'm not sure what kind of cologne he uses but love the way it smells. I remember the day I held his hoodie to my face to smell it. This is way better. Something about the rocking of the boat and the warmth of his embrace lulls me to sleep. I wake with a start when he nibbles on my ear. It takes me a moment to understand where I am, and then my eyes snap to his shirt to make sure I've not done something embarrassing like drool on him. Thankfully, I have not.

"We should be heading back."

"Why? Let's just stay out here."

"Not tonight. But maybe we can sail one weekend somewhere."

"I'd like that."

His lips move to my neck. "Now that I've woken you. I don't want to go back."

"Then don't."

"Would you really like to sleep out here?"

I turn and look up at the sky. It's like I've never seen it before. So clear and full of stars, but as warm as Ryan is, it is getting chilly.

"It is a bit cold, but it's so beautiful."

"It's warmer in the cabin. There's a bed down there if you'd like to sleep on the boat tonight."

"Where will you sleep?"

"I'll be fine up here with some blankets."

"Would you like to go in the cabin with me?"

"I don't want you to feel pressured to do anything."

"I don't. I just like the idea of falling asleep in your arms. Besides, we've slept in the same room before."

"But not the same bed."

"I know."

"You sure?"

I sit up and pull him with me below deck. The door to the cabin is just past the bathroom. In the room is a platform-styled queen bed with a thick blue comforter on it. I slip off my sandals and lay back on the bed as he slowly closes the door behind him, watching me. I scoot back to the pillows and pull the comforter from underneath me to cover myself. Once I'm settled, he lays down next to me but on top of the covers.

"Ryan, come on. Get under the covers."

He groans, sitting up to kick off his shoes before joining me. Even though I was tired before, the idea that I'm lying in a bed with him has me wired awake, and considering how chilly it is outside, it's getting stuffy in here. Ryan must feel that way as well. He sits up to slide open two small circular windows that are on either side of the cabin to allow the air to circulate. I push the comforter down, and he pulls me into his arms. His kisses are urgent, and his hands are buried in my hair. I cling to him as he lowers me onto the bed and covers me with his body.

My hands wrap around his back, and I pull him closer to me. I start tugging on his shirt, wanting to feel his skin. He sits up and pulls it and the t-shirt he wears under it off.

Before he lays back down, I bring my hands up to his chest. He's on the lean side, but his muscles are defined in a way that's making my mouth water. His shoulders and biceps are rock hard, and I know it's from all of the lifting and kayaking he does at work. He has an amused expression on his face as I explore the contours of his body.

"What?" I ask, catching his eye.

He shrugs, a very mischievous look on his face. "Just looking forward to my turn."

I blush, turning to hide my face in a pillow.

"Had not meant for that to be a scary thing." He playfully tugs on my arm. "Grace, I'm not in any hurry. Well, truthfully, I'd love for stuff to happen sooner rather than the alternative. What I'm trying to say is never, ever feel rushed with me, okay? And I promise to sit on my hands if you want to touch me again because that felt heavenly."

I peek up at him before sitting back up, bringing my hands to touch him again. I hear him sharply inhale when I lean down to kiss his chest. When I look back up at him, he captures my mouth with his. A moan escapes my lips, and Ryan pulls back. I look at him, confused.

"Just need a minute. Scratch that, Maybe an hour."

I lie back against the pillows and bite the knuckle of my index finger to hold back a laugh. It's hard not to feel giddy looking at this beautiful man and knowing the effect I am having on him. It makes me feel dizzy and amazed that this is actually happening. Knowing how he is seals it for me; how he flew to Cleveland to help me move down here; how he takes care of Kate. I picture the sweet little grannies gushing over him at the knitting club. When I had fallen in love with Jon, there was this bad boy appeal to him. He'd talked me into ditching the date I was on to be with him. It had been exciting, but when times got rough, he'd taken it out on me.

Ryan doesn't need to act like that. There is no reason for him to be aggressive or a bully. Like when those lawyers made a pass at me. He had not yelled or threatened them, just said I was his girlfriend and that was that. I know, though, just as he had said above on the deck, that he will protect me.

He swings his legs over the side of the bed. On my knees, I move over to him and begin gently kissing his back.

"Ryan?"

He turns to look at me.

"What if I don't want to wait?"

I grab his hand and pull him back to me before unhooking my belt and dropping it over the side of the bed. Then I take his hands and place them on the hem of my shirt and lift my arms up in the air for him to pull it off of me. He leans down to kiss the swell of my breasts as I reach behind to unclasp my bra. When it is unhooked, he slowly slides it from me.

"Are you sure?"

I nod, inching closer to him. He takes me in his arms, and the sensation of his bare chest on mine is amazing. He lowers me to the bed and eases my skirt down my legs until it joins the pile of clothes on the cabin floor. He then explores my body with his mouth and hands. I learn what it means to be cherished. He asks me over and over if I'm sure, so cautious about crossing a line with me. It gets to the point where I finally beg him to take me. He makes short work of the rest of his clothes after that. He panics momentarily, looking for a condom and then checks the expiration of it once he finds one. He shrugs, admitting it has been a while. In fact, the condom is probably Darrell's. I don't care. I'm just relieved he's able to find one.

Ryan makes love to me on that boat as it rocks in the

Gulf of Mexico and the fresh sea air drifts through the windows. In the end, as we lay in a panting tangle of arms and legs, I feel wonderful, worshipped. He pulls me closer to him and tucks a loose strand of hair behind my ear before kissing me. We fall asleep like that. The next morning, when I wake up in his arms, I look up to see him grinning down at me.

He kisses my forehead. "I did not expect that to happen."

I run my nose over his earlobe. "Happy?"

"Thrilled. Except for the fact that you'll be sleeping next door and not in my arms tonight."

"I can sleep over if you'd like."

"I'd like that very much. I think we should head back before Kate starts to worry."

We both slowly dress. Ryan uses the bathroom first before heading up to pull the anchor. I find a tube of toothpaste in the bathroom and use my finger to brush my teeth as best as I can before going to join him. He hasn't put his dress shirt back on. Watching him steer the boat in his khakis and undershirt is such a turn on. I walk over and wrap my arms around his waist. He reaches around and pulls me in front of him, kissing the back of my head. He steers with one hand, the other pulling me to him. I bring both of my arms to hold his arm tighter to my chest.

When we get closer to the dock, Ryan uses the hook end of the long wooden pole he had used to push us from the dock the night before. He has me hold the pole while he jumps onto the dock and ties the boat to two posts. I help him collect our things and the trash from the boat before he helps me off. Walking back up the hill towards his car, I try to wrap my brain around the fact that I had just made love on a boat with the Adonis standing beside me. He drives most of the way with one hand on my thigh, lazily rubbing his thumb back and forth. He parks in front of Kate's house and walks me to the door. I had meant to give him a sweet peck before I walk in, but he deepens it, pulling me to him.

"Do you want me to come in with you?"

"Don't be silly. Besides, you probably have Jack wondering where you are."

He kisses me again before turning to walk home. I slip inside and go to find Kate, going first to the lanai. When I walk in, I'm surprised to see Jack eating breakfast with Kate. And here I am, strolling in and wearing my clothes from last night. The look Jack gives me makes me blush further.

"Hi, Kate. Hello, Jack. Um, just wanted to let you know I was home."

"Sit, dear. We want to hear all about your date."

"Is it okay if I take a quick shower first?"

"Feeling dirty?" Jack grins at me.

"Shut it, mate." Ryan walks in behind me and kisses my cheek.

"I thought you were going home."

"Figured Jack came over here."

"Why don't you hang out with them? I'd really like to change."

"Of course." He kisses me sweetly, and I head to my room.

I take a quick shower, throwing on a polo and some shorts, then brush my teeth and hair before going back out to the pool deck. Kate is knitting while Ryan tells them about our date. When I walk in, Jack is questioning my choice of burger toppings.

"It's really good," I argue.

"Still sounds gross."

"Then don't eat it."

"Trust me, I won't."

"So did you stay on the boat all night?" Kate asks.

I look at Ryan.

"Well, I know they didn't come back to Ryan's place."

"Yes, we spent the night on the boat. That's enough about that. Kate, how was your evening?" I say, picking up my knitting.

We all sit around chatting after that, Jack unsuccessfully tries to steer the conversation back to what happened on our date a couple of times. Before long, Ryan and Jack leave. Ryan needs a shower, and Jack is actually in town to check out some real estate.

Kissing me on the cheek, Ryan whispers. "Did you still want to spend the night tonight?"

I nod, blushing. The grin he gives me makes me blush even more. I push him away, laughing. I think he's left when he hurries back into the room to give me another kiss before leaving.

"That boy is smitten with you."

"You think so?"

"Yes, Grace. I'm certain, and I do believe you feel the same way."

"I do. I feel a bit weird, like it is too soon since I stopped seeing Jon. Did I tell you he texted me that he missed me? How strange is that? As strange as that makes me feel, I can't deny how I feel about Ryan."

"Ryan is wonderful. I can see why you like him."

"But I think I more than like him. What if he doesn't more than like me?"

"I wouldn't worry about that, dear. I'm pretty sure he more than likes you."

"I hope you're right."

"You just dropped a stitch, and I know I'm right."

I look down at my knitting. "Will you help me get it back?"

Kate fixes my dropped stitch then pats me on the knee.

"Do you think these are good enough to sell like Jack said?"

"I've seen the stuff they sell in the stores. I know many people prefer handmade. I do. Is this something you would like to do?"

"I don't know. Maybe."

"I would be sure about it before you do."

"I feel like it would be really cool to be my own boss, not that I don't like working with Ryan. I do. It's just that now that we're going out on dates—"

"And having sleepovers."

I flush. "And, er, having sleepovers. Will it be weird that he's my boss?"

"I don't know. I can see if you only knew him that way but you haven't, and I believe this has been brewing for a while."

"I just keep thinking about it and how cool it would be. I've seen all of these cool things I could try and make. You know, like those scarves that attach at the ends, or maybe hats. Do you think I could make hats?"

"Hats are easy and don't take very long to make, but won't you be busy spending time with Ryan?"

"I'm sure I will, but maybe I could do this too. I'm getting faster, and I don't have to look down at my hands as much."

"Well, you seem very comfortable making scarves. Why don't I teach you how to make a hat when you are done with that one, and what ever happened to the shawl you were working on?"

I set my knitting down and tell Kate I will be right back. Now is the perfect time to give it to her because it's just the two of us. I hurry to my room to retrieve it. I have it neatly folded and tied with wide white ribbon around it. I hug it to my chest as I walk back onto the lanai.

"Kate?" My voice is shaking.

"Yes, dear?"

"I made this for you. I don't have much, and you gave me the one thing that I didn't think I would ever have again: family. I know things were strained with you and my mom. I just wish more than anything that she would have moved past it before, well. It's just that you have come to mean so much to me, to do so much for me."

Kate reaches out to grab one of my hands. I wipe away a tear with the other.

"I'm happier than I've ever been, and I want you to know it's because of you. I can't imagine what you went through, losing Ronny and then my mom. When you explained that the purpose of the shawl was to give comfort," I struggle to finish. "I just wanted to do something to give you comfort."

"Come here, child." Kate pats the seat next to her, and once I sit, Kate pulls me into a gentle hug. "Grace, when you called me that day and said that you would come and see me, that was the greatest gift anyone has ever given me. You didn't know me. That day, you gave me a family as well. I would be honored to accept your gift."

I stand only to go grab a box of tissues from the house.

"Aren't we a mess?" Kate laughs, pulling an extra one from the box.

I nod, wiping my eyes.

"Hello." Ryan walks in, then sees us crying. "What's wrong?"

"Oh, don't mind us, dear. Grace just gave me a lovely gift so I'm being sentimental."

I stand, and he gives me a hug. "I'm just trying to thank her for taking me in."

He rests his chin on top of my head and holds me tight. "I should probably be thanking her as well, for bringing you to me."

"Don't you make me cry too, young man. Why don't you take Grace out for an ice cream?"

He bends his knees, lowering himself to eye level with me. "Sound good?"

I nod, then turn back to Kate. "Can we bring you back some?"

"Twist my arm."

I lean down to kiss her cheek. "Will do."

Walking together to Ryan's Jeep, I can't help but notice how perfectly my hand fits in his. He walks me to the passenger side door, leaning me against it. Taking his thumbs, he gently wipes the moisture away from below my eyes. I close my eyes and let my hands sit on the waist band of his shorts as he presses soft kisses on my forehead, cheeks, nose, and lastly, lips. I open my eyes before he pulls away and become lost in his gaze. His smile is infectious. As we stand there, inches apart, I feel so exhilarated. Reaching my hands up to his neck, I pull him in for another deeper kiss. His lips, his touch, him. I want to lose myself in all of it.

Breaking our kiss, Ryan looks slightly dazed when he pulls back. "If we don't stop, I'm going to throw you over my shoulder and take you to my bed."

I hide my face in his shirt. That's exactly what I want to do. But there's Kate. "How about we go get ice cream, and once Kate lies down this afternoon, we do that."

"Really?" He can't keep the excitement out of his voice.

"Mm hm."

He leans down to kiss me again, pulling me towards him as he backs away from the car and reaches behind me to open my door before taking his lips from mine. I slide into my seat, resting my hands on my knees as he shuts my door. While we drive to the ice cream parlor, I tell Ryan I'm interested in maybe trying to open my own Etsy store. Ryan thinks it's brilliant and promises to help in any way he can. The ice cream parlor he takes me to has a drive thru. Since we're bringing back ice cream for Kate, we use it. Ryan picks up three hand-packed pints: French Vanilla for Kate, Chocolate Raspberry Truffle for me, and Mint Chocolate Chip for himself.

They give us plastic spoons with our order, and I consider starting mine right away but figure I can wait until we get back to the house. Eating ice cream instead of lunch around the pool is a guilty pleasure we all enjoy indulging in. When Kate goes to lie down, Ryan looks at me mischievously. My stomach flips. Why am I so nervous all of a sudden? I felt so confident earlier out by his car. I can tell he is trying to figure out what I want to do. Why am I even nervous? I want him, and I know he wants me too. I stand and reach out my hand to him.

Ryan pulls me into his lap, his hands molded to my hips, kissing me hungrily as if my lips are the only possible relief for his hunger. I tangle my fingers in his hair, gasping when he lifts me and carries me out the back door and across the yard to his house.

"I…can…walk," I breathe between kisses.

His lips move to my neck as he replies, "Not a chance."

Entering by the side door, he pulls back enough to shout, "Jack!" a couple times, then looking back at my confused look, "Just wanted to make sure he isn't here."

He nudges the door to his bedroom open with his foot and kicks it closed behind us. Claiming my mouth once more, he eases me onto his bed. I tug at his shirt, and pausing for a beat, he pulls it off. He lies down next to me, pulling me on top of him. Our clothes are shed and heaped on the floor by the bed in moments. I feel timid about my body. It had been so dark on the boat the night before. This feels more intimate, like there is no part of me I can hide. Ryan takes his time exploring my every curve. When I feel like I can't take it any longer, he reaches for a condom.

Locking eyes as he sinks into me, Ryan groans. I giggle at his expression. He playfully nips at my chin before rocking his hips against mine. It's no laughing matter when he lifts my leg to his shoulder. I twist my hands into the pillows behind me, arching to meet him over and over again. Sitting up, his hands are vices on my hips, setting a pace that ignites something within me. Feeling I'm close, he leans back down to cover me, and I wrap my legs around his waist. Placing one hand on either side of my face, his lips find mine, and I cling to him as I come undone. He collapses on top of me only moments later.

"So beautiful." He dances soft kisses all over my face.

"This doesn't even seem real."

"Very real." He moves to kissing the tops of my shoulders.

"Like too good to be true."

"Nope. Just the right amount of good and very true."

"You are so silly."

"And you are heavenly."

"How is it possible that you didn't have a girlfriend when we met?"

He leans back, resting his head on his hand, fingertips of his other hand drawing lazy circles on my thigh. "I've never been much of a going out guy. When I moved here, I was so busy with the business and became such good friends with Kate I just wasn't in a position to meet many girls."

"Do you like me just because I'm around?" I say it jokingly but am insecure in his feelings for me.

"The very first moment I saw you, Grace, in the airport, I thought who is this blue eyed, blonde goddess, and what must I do to make her mine? I was very bothered when I learned you had a fella, but you were so amazing I figured you could not be single."

"Hush."

"Do you miss him?"

I pull Ryan to me. "I miss what we had, but that was long gone before I met you."

"I'm very happy you feel that way," he says before covering my mouth with his.

Epilogue

It's been seven months since our date on the boat. I've stopped applying to other places, content to work with Ryan. My ease in the office takes a lot of pressure off and lets him concentrate leading tours and managing the equipment. He talked me into moving in with him full time months ago. We still have dinner almost every night at Kate's. She's been teaching me how to knit different things. Figuring out how to use circular needles was not fun.

I now know how to make hats, infinity scarves, leg warmers, and fingerless gloves. The idea of an Etsy store ignited something in me the moment Jack suggested it. I spend my free time researching other stores to get an idea of what's successful and what isn't, I'm not very tech savvy, but Jennifer loves that kind of stuff, and during down time at work, explains different websites and how they can work together to save me time. One example is creating a Facebook entity page and linking it to a Twitter page. Whatever is posted on the Facebook page can automatically post to Twitter. One post, two websites.

Jennifer is also helping me design a theme to use for my

Etsy page. It isn't live yet, but I've created an account. It took me some time to decide what to name my store. I finally decided on Cuyahoga Knits as a way to include my parents in my present. The idea came to me one day while Ryan and I were driving into work. He had the radio on an 80s station and an REM song I'd never heard came on. I couldn't believe what I was hearing: a song about the Cuyahoga. I turned up the volume, listening to the lyrics. I grew up in Cleveland, so I knew Cuyahoga was an Indian term for crooked, a perfect description of the many bends of the river.

The song spoke of preserving what we have before it's too late. It felt symbolic of the relationship I'd built with Kate. I've learned so much about her, my mother, and myself in coming down here. I'm still learning so many things every day. There was a point during the creation of the Etsy store account that made me reflective. Just after hitting the submit button an additional warning came up. Are you sure?

Am I sure? I wondered to myself. So many things have changed in my life: the visit, then the move, Kate, Ryan, and learning to knit. Am I sure about any of it? No more hesitation, I'm sure, no matter what happens.

I smile and look at Ryan sleeping next to me.

"Honey, wake up," I nudge his shoulder.

He mumbles something and crawls onto me, nibbling my neck.

Oh, that feels good. "But our flight."

His hips press against mine, and I'm gone. I wrap my arms around his neck and pull his lips down to mine. It's a good thing I set our alarm thirty minutes early. After Ryan has thoroughly ravished me, I convince him to take a shower while I double-check my bags for the hundredth time. He calls from the bathroom once he's out of the shower. I pause in the doorway to admire him. He's shaving. I don't mind him scruffy, but he wants to look nice today. He catches my eye in the mirror and winks.

I hurry into the shower, patting him on the rear as I pass. Once I'm ready, I help Ryan and Jennifer load our bags into her car. Her only request for taking us to and picking us up from the airport is to be allowed to boss Darrell around while we're gone. Ryan agreed since she'll do it whether he tells her she can or not.

My stomach is a bundle of nerves on the way to the airport. Ryan's a pro, getting our bags checked and us through security. We eat breakfast at the gate and are in the first group to board.

Once we're seated, Ryan looks at me. "Are you alright?"

I turn to face Ryan and nod. I'm nervous. Not only are we on our way to meet his family, but the only other time I've flown anywhere was to Tampa. For this trip, we have two layovers, one in Dallas and the second in Sydney, before ending up in Christchurch. We're going to be in the air for over twenty-two hours from Dallas to Sydney. That alone is overwhelming. Getting my passport was an ordeal but now that we're seated, I'm trying to relax.

Besides worrying about the flight, I'm stressing about meeting Ryan's family. I want them to like me. Ryan thinks I'm silly to even worry, but I can't help it. Kate is my entire family, and she had already adored him before we even met. I lift the window shade and look out. Since our journey will be so long, Ryan had sprung for first class seats. I think the expense is too much, but he wants us (me) to be comfortable. He hopes we can sleep most of the way to Australia. Ryan reaches over to take my hand in his and kisses it. I can't help but smile at him. He's so excited about taking me to his home.

Kate has a theory he's going to propose on the trip. If he does, I know I'll say yes. I just can't imagine my life without him. Once we're back from New Zealand, I plan on inviting Nikita down for a visit to see my new home.

For me, waking up in Ryan's arms everyday has been a dream. We still have dinner most nights with Kate since neither of us is much of a cook. Samuel, a widower from her church, has been joining us recently. Kate won't admit it, but I think she really likes him. I can't wait to hear how their dinners go while Ryan and I are away.

I reach into my carryon to pull out my latest project. Ryan didn't believe me when I told him you can carry on knitting needles. I checked online to be sure and packed wooden needles just in case.

He leans over to kiss my cheek. I pause to look at him, my Ryan. My life is so different now. My path to where I am today was not easy, but sitting here, next to the man I love, the man who has become my partner and who challenges me to go after what I want in life, I know I'm where I'm supposed be.

"Is this real?" I tease.

He leans down, kisses my forehead, and says, "Yes Grace, very real."

The End

Keep reading for the first chapter of Him, the first book in my Him & Her series. Available Now!

Join my mailing list to learn about FREE books and fun giveaways at www.CareyHeywood.com

Him

ONE

- Present -

After closing the refrigerator door, I pause, juice in hand, to look at my brother's wedding invitation. It's held up by a local pizza place's magnet and I've looked at it at least a hundred times. I should probably start packing. I'm normally so good at it, always prepared in advance for whatever trip I'm taking. This time is different, I'm headed home. When I got the save the date card a year ago, I called my brother, the groom. I tried to sell Brian on the idea of a destination wedding. Someplace tropic, Aruba or maybe Cabo. No, his fiancée, Christine was set on Decatur, our hometown. Something about dreaming about getting married in the little white church there and having all of her friends and family with her. Ugh.

There is no getting out of going, kind of a requirement of being a sibling. Plus, Christine, the bride, wants me to be a bridesmaid. At least the bridesmaid dresses are pretty, I picture the pale blue dress hanging in my closet. I take a sip of my drink as I walk into the living room. Our condo has an amazing view of the Rockies from the picture window in the living room. Sawyer has her mat laid out in a patch of sunlight in our living room and is going through a series of yoga poses. I sit on the sofa, waiting for her to finish.

After ending in a final child's pose, she turns to me, her gray blue eyes bright. She rolls up her mat before joining me on the sofa, tucking her legs under her as she sits.

"Dude, have you packed yet?"

"Dude?" I cock my head at her. "You never say dude."

She blushes. Sawyer also never blushes.

I pick up a pillow and throw it at her and laugh. "But I know somebody who does!"

"Don't change the subject." She avoids what I've said altogether. "Packed yet?"

I flop back onto the arm of the sofa. "No, I haven't." I groan. "I don't want to go."

I know I'm whining, but I really don't want to go. She stands, holding out her hand to help me off of the sofa, which is laughable considering how much smaller she is than me. "Stop being a wuss." I let her pull me up. "I'll help you pack."

"Fine," I grumble and follow her, my shoulders slumped the whole way to my room.

I tried packing last night and had gotten only as far as pulling down my shiny red rolling suitcase. It still stands, proudly, next to my closet. I lift it and lay it open across my bed. Sawyer buzzes around me, throwing stuff into it.

"I don't think I'll need so many dresses," I argue.

"You never know. Maybe you'll hook up with a groomsman."

I pick up one of the dresses she's flung in my suitcase and neatly refold it. "Unlikely. All but one are married or already have girlfriends."

She smirks, lifting a brow.

"What?" I shrug my shoulders. "I asked Brian last time

I talked to him. Even asked him the name of the only single guy, but he had to hang up before he could tell me."

"Why? Were you planning on practicing doodling his name on your binder?"

I roll my eyes. "I don't do that."

"Right, Sarah. Your last *real* relationship was in high school. Can you repeat after me? High school." She uses air quotes.

"I've dated," I argue weakly.

She gives me a look like, really?

But I'm gaining speed. "Yeah, remember that guy? What was his name? The one who had the three legged dog."

She nods. "That was a really cute dog. If I remember correctly, you spent more time with Rover than Jeremy. And why do I remember the name of the guy you dated and you don't?"

I look away. "Did not."

She keeps going. "So why did you stop seeing Jeremy?"

I lie. "I forget."

Sawyer's always been able to tell when I lie. "Liar! You stopped seeing him because he flossed! Who does that? Who thinks flossing is a con?" she says in disbelief.

"You know that's not why. It's not that he flossed. I like that he flossed. It's that he had to tell me every time he was going to go floss. Why? Why did he do that? Was he trying to prove something? Hey, look at me." I wave my hands in the air. "I'm going to go floss now!"

Sawyer throws a pair of socks at my head. "He was a dentist. You are a crazy person."

I turn to pick up the socks from the floor and put them in the inside pocket of my suitcase "He just wasn't for me." I grin, looking up. "I would've kept his dog, though. His name was Tank by the way."

Sawyer brings my bridesmaid dress out of the closet and sets it on top of everything else, folding it in the middle. "I'm worried about you."

I freeze. "Why?"

She shakes her head. "I know you, and I want you to know I am so proud of everything you have accomplished. But."

I raise a brow. "But?"

She takes a deep breath. "But you are using your job as a reason to not cultivate human relationships."

"What? Human relationships? What are you, a robot?"

"Don't argue. Besides, I predate your company. I'm grandfathered or whatever. And, besides me, who do you talk to or hang out with?"

I spin my ring. "I met Jared for lunch, like…"

She laughs. "Sarah, you had lunch with Jared six months ago. We're going out tonight."

"I can't." I groan. "I have to fly out early. I have that lumber yard account to set up before I go home."

"You aren't flying straight home?"

"No." I shrug. "It's work."

"You need to hire someone else to cut your workload down. This is too much for one person, babe."

"I'm fine. I can do it."

She cuts me off. "Yeah, 'cause then you couldn't hide behind your job anymore. We're still going out tonight. I'll have you home early."

"Why is this such a big deal?"

"Sarah, when was the last time you had sex?"

"I'm not sleeping with anyone tonight."

"Geez, dude, you need to loosen up."

"Ah ha! You just said dude again."

She waves me off, walking back into my closet and

pulling out a green dress. "Go shower and wear this." She sets it on my bed before walking out of my room.

I'm drying my hair when she comes back to check on my progress. Taking my brush from me, she starts playing with my hair. Hair has always been her thing. When I first met her, she had multiple pastel-shaded streaks. I think she's always wished I would let her dye my hair. I, on the other hand, am happy with my brown hair. She braids a chunk of it and pins it like a headband across the top of my head. We head to her car, a Hummer. It always makes me laugh because Sawyer is tiny and her car is huge.

We head to a nearby restaurant bar. There is a live band playing. As we're seated, I notice the bassist nod in Sawyer's direction. "Know him?"

"Oh, that's James. He's cool. He's the one who lives part-time in France. We went out a couple times."

Our server comes by to take our drink orders. Once he's gone, she looks up from her menu. "What are you going to get?"

I shrug. "Clam cakes, or Chicken Kiev. Haven't decided. You?"

"The Portobello Mushroom Pasta looks good. Hey, I forgot to ask where's this lumber yard you're setting up?"

"Just outside Newark. I wonder if anyone we know still lives out there. Helen moved to San Diego."

"Jake's still out there. Want his number? I'm sure he'd meet up for lunch or dinner."

I grin. She's the only person I've ever met who is on good terms with all of her exes. "I'm not going to be there long enough to hang out. Gotta get in, get out, and get to Atlanta."

We order and hang out until our food arrives. The band takes a break, and James and another guy come over to sit with us. As close as James is sitting to Sawyer, I wonder if he hopes they'll hang out later tonight as well. His band mate, the drummer, is named Trent and seems nice enough. They get up once our food comes to go play some more.

"So what'd you think of Trent?"

I hold up my hand as I finish my bite. "He seemed nice."

Her eyes widen. "You don't think he's hot?"

I glance back over to the stage. "I guess. He sure wears a lot of black."

She laughs at me. "Sweetheart, you could find an issue with any guy. Is anyone ever going to be good enough for you?"

I spin my ring, trying not to think about the blue eyes that owned me. "Someday," I hedge. "Who knows."

We have another drink and stay to listen to the band for another hour before heading home. They are still on stage as we leave, and Sawyer catches James' eye as we are walking out and waving bye. I go right to bed when we get home, wondering if Sawyer will have company once James is done playing. She is something. Part of me wishes I could live like she does, so free. Everyone who meets her loves her. God, when Brian came out to visit once, I thought he was going to ask her out. That would have been just weird. He still asks how she's doing every time we talk. She has that effect on people. I, on the other hand, do not. There are no ex-boyfriends trying to track me down. I fall asleep trying to think of anything other than my first love.

Acknowledgments

I want to thank everyone who helped and encouraged me along this journey. To my first readers, Judy Greco, Kate Dixon (ahem, inspiration for the Segway fall), Amy Surrey, Angelique Miller (your pictures of Cleveland made my month!), Kristy Jamieson, Sarah Stevenson, Elly Ruzgal, and Stephanie Crews.

Gareth Young, I don't know where to start. You are one of the most giving people I have ever met. Thank you so much for your time and devotion to contractions.

Vanessa Brown, you are not only Physic but Psychic too!

Kristina Radi, my Etsy guru. You are an incredibly talented knitter, and a beautiful person. Thank you for letting me pick your brain. Your feedback was invaluable. Find her site at: www.etsy.com/shop/AutumnAndAmber

Yesenia Vargas, I trust you with my words. You are not only my editor, but my friend.

To Melodie Ramone, Nikki Mahood, Helen Boswell, Rachel Walter, Emma Hart, and Ross McCoubrey, your friendship and support mean so much to me.

To all of the blogs/Facebook pages that have given me so much love, thank you.

Lastly, to Seth, Zach, Aydan, and Emma for being okay with cereal for dinner sometimes, and dealing with my crazy full time.

About the Author

New York Times and USA Today bestselling romance author. She was born and raised in Alexandria, Virginia. Supporting her all the way are her husband, three sometimes-adorable children, a mischievous black cat, and their nine-pound attack Yorkie.

She loves to hear from her readers!

www.CareyHeywood.com
info@CareyHeywood.com

Also by Carey Heywood

Him & Her Series

Him (book 1)

Her (book 2)

Them (book 3)

Sawyer Says (spin off)

Being Neighborly (spin off novella)

Carolina Days

The Other Side of Someday (Courtney & Clay)

Yesterday's Half Truths (Lindsay & Luke)

Chasing Daylight (McKenzie & Mitch)

Love Riddles

Why Now? (Kacey & Jake)

Why Lie? (Sydney & Heath)

Why Not? (Reilly & Trip)

Standalones

Better

Stages of Grace

Uninvolved

A Bridge of Her Own

Audiobooks

Him (also available on audible)

Her (also available on audible)

Better (also available on audible)

www.ingramcontent.com/pod-product-compliance
Lightning Source LLC
LaVergne TN
LVHW010652110826
845149LV00014B/3049

* 9 7 8 0 9 8 8 7 7 1 3 4 5 *